**'I think you mistake.'**

'A mistake?'

'It wouldn't work.'

He feigned innocence. 'Why on earth not?'

'You really need to ask?' Lady Caterina grimaced as she elaborated, 'We're not even capable of conducting a civil conversation. How on earth could we possibly contemplate working together?'

Matthew smiled. 'Think of it as a challenge.'

Caterina did not smile back. 'There are challenges and challenges. And this one, I'm afraid, just doesn't appeal to me.'

**Dear Reader,**

Welcome to Royal Affair! By appointment to her loyal readers, Stephanie Howard has created a blue-blooded trilogy of Romeos, rebels and royalty. It follows the fortunes of the San Rinaldo royal family: Damiano, the Duke of San Rinaldo, his brother, Count Leone, and their sister, Lady Caterina. Together the three of them are dedicated to their country, people and family. But it takes only one thing to turn their perfectly ordered lives upside down: love!

COUNT LEONE MONTECRESPI, the younger brother of the ruling Duke, was a habitual heartbreaker. A playboy of the old school: love them, leave them and on no account marry them. But would small-town American girl Carrie Dunn be the one to finally get him up the aisle?

LADY CATERINA MONTECRESPI, Leone and Damiano's baby sister, had sworn off men since her last disastrous encounter with the opposite sex. And Matthew Allenby was hardly the man to change her mind. As far as Caterina was concerned, he was a crook and a charlatan. Unfortunately he was also proving irresistible!

The DUKE OF SAN RINALDO, DAMIANO MONTECRESPI, had married Sofia to secure his dukedom and produce an heir. But duty for Sofia was a cold bed partner–she wanted Damiano to love her as much as he did their baby son, Alessandro. Was a happy ending to their fairy-tale romance too much to ask for?

Each of these books contains its own stand-alone romance as well as making up a great trilogy. Follow Leone and Carrie's tale in THE COLORADO COUNTESS. In THE LADY'S MAN it's the turn of Caterina and Matthew. And finally THE DUKE'S WIFE features Sofia and Damiano's story–not forgetting little baby Alessandro!

With three royal weddings and a baby, this is one series you don't want to miss!

Happy reading!

*The Editor*

# THE LADY'S MAN

BY
STEPHANIE HOWARD

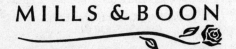

> **DID YOU PURCHASE THIS BOOK WITHOUT A COVER?**
> If you did, you should be aware it is **stolen property** as it was reported
> *unsold and destroyed* by a retailer. Neither the author nor the publisher
> has received any payment for this book.

*All the characters in this book have no existence outside the imagination of the author, and have no relation whatsoever to anyone bearing the same name or names. They are not even distantly inspired by any individual known or unknown to the author, and all the incidents are pure invention.*

*All rights reserved including the right of reproduction in whole or in part in any form. This edition is published by arrangement with Harlequin Enterprises II B.V. The text of this publication or any part thereof may not be reproduced or transmitted in any form or by any means, electronic or mechanical, including photocopying, recording, storage in an information retrieval system, or otherwise, without the written permission of the publisher.*

*This book is sold subject to the condition that it shall not, by way of trade or otherwise, be lent, resold, hired out or otherwise circulated without the prior consent of the publisher in any form of binding or cover other than that in which it is published and without a similar condition including this condition being imposed on the subsequent purchaser.*

*MILLS & BOON and the Rose Device
are trademarks of the publisher.
Harlequin Mills & Boon Limited,
Eton House, 18-24 Paradise Road, Richmond, Surrey TW9 1SR*

© Stephanie Howard 1996

ISBN 0 263 79515 2

*Set in Times Roman 10½ on 12 pt.
01-9606-51930 C1*

*Made and printed in Great Britain*

**Stephanie Howard** was born and brought up in Dundee in Scotland, and educated at the London School of Economics. For ten years she worked as a journalist in London on a variety of women's magazines, among them *Woman's Own,* and was latterly editor of the now defunct *Honey.* She has spent many years living and working abroad—in Italy, Malaysia, the Philippines and in the Middle East.

**Recent titles by the same author:**

THE BEST FOR LAST
THE MAN WHO BROKE HEARTS
THE COLORADO COUNTESS

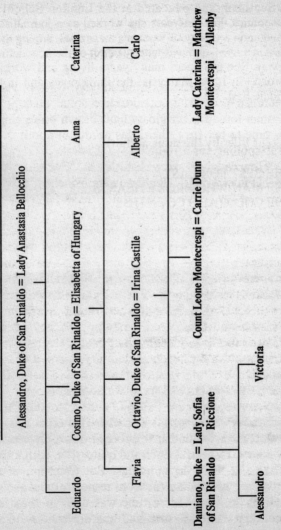

# CHAPTER ONE

CATERINA was furious. White-knuckle furious. As she marched down the corridor like some unstoppable human tornado, her glossy light brown bob swinging in time to her fury, there was no doubt about it, she was spoiling for a fight.

'How dare he?' she was muttering. 'I've had enough of his interfering!' Her fists were clenched, her blue eyes sparking. 'Well, this time I'm putting my foot down! He's not getting away with it!'

Luckily the corridor down which she was marching was empty. The only eyes and ears to bear witness to her tirade were the unseeing, unhearing ones depicted in the portraits—of bishops and princes and generals of old—that hung in their carved frames from the silk-upholstered walls. For the corridor in question was the splendid west-wing corridor of the fabulous Palazzo Verde, home for three hundred years of the illustrious Montecrespis, hereditary rulers of the little dukedom of San Rinaldo—the west wing being where the current Duke had his private quarters.

Generally, it must be said, visitors to the Duke's private office—for that was where Caterina was currently headed—tended to proceed down the corridor at a more respectful pace and quite often with a sense of awe at their surroundings. But Caterina, at this moment, was feeling far from respectful and she was unlikely to be awed for she was used to these surroundings. For the man she was on her way to see,

His Grace, the Duke of San Rinaldo, just so happened to be her brother.

Not that her feelings right now were particularly sisterly either. As she reached the panelled door that led to his office, she flung it open impatiently and strode across the threshold.

'Damiano!' she bellowed. 'I've got a bone to pick with you!'

The only person in the room, however, was Rosa, Damiano's pretty young secretary. She'd been sitting at her desk, quietly working at her word processor, but she leapt to her feet now like a poor startled frog.

'Lady Caterina, I'm sorry,' she started to explain, curtsying, 'but I'm afraid His Grace isn't here at the moment.'

Normally Caterina would have chastised her for curtsying, for she had told her a hundred times that it really wasn't necessary. But right now she had other, more pressing matters on her mind.

'Isn't here?' She swept furiously across the huge room, totally disregarding what Rosa had just told her, and thrust her head round the door of his private inner office. 'He's got to be here! I made an appointment!'

But, appointment or not, there was definitely no Damiano, though Caterina continued to stand in the doorway for a moment, her china-blue eyes angrily scouring every corner as though she might detect him hiding under the carpet.

'Damn him!' she muttered. 'He knew I was coming!'

Then she turned back to Rosa, scowling like a gorgon. 'Where has he gone? What's going on here? Why didn't somebody let me know?'

Poor Rosa, who took pride in being the very soul of efficiency and who had never seen Caterina in such a ferocious mood before—the Duke's twenty-five-year-old sister was normally easygoing and friendly—blushed in dismay at this implicit accusation.

'I—I don't know, m'lady,' she stuttered. 'I wasn't told anything. I—'

But that was as far as she got. She was stopped in her tracks as a male voice said, 'Don't worry about it, Rosa. I'll take charge of things from here.'

The two young women turned as one in the direction of the speaker, who was standing in the doorway that led from the west-wing corridor. And as their eyes fell on his dark, commanding figure one of them smiled and one of them did not.

The one who did not was Caterina. Well, one didn't generally smile at the sudden appearance of a viper, and a viper was precisely what Caterina saw as she looked, with a rush of loathing, into Matthew Allenby's face.

If he was a viper, however, he was a viper with biceps, for Matthew Allenby positively exuded ruthless power. Tall and muscularly built, he possessed an arrogant self-assurance that shone, as sharp as a razor, from the iron-grey eyes. Eyes that could stop you in your tracks with just the force of a single glance.

He could also stop you in your tracks just with the way he looked. For, as even Caterina would not have denied, he really was quite outrageously attractive. Dark hair, thick and glossy, wide, sensual mouth, the lines of his tanned face sculpted and powerful. And he had an aura of danger and mystery about him that most women, Caterina suspected, found irresistibly seductive.

Most women, that was, very definitely excluding her! Though as she looked at him now and he met her eyes and smiled at her with that habitual air of casual superiority she felt, as always, the threat of the danger that lurked in him and knew it would be wise to keep him safely at arm's length. She loathed him but she found him deeply unsettling.

She flicked him a cool look. 'So you plan on taking charge? Well, I'm sorry, Mr Allenby, but you'll be doing no such thing.'

'Forgive me, Lady Caterina, but I rather think I will.'

As he addressed her, as protocol demanded he inclined his head slightly, but the amused, superior smile not for one moment left his face. He had this knack, as Caterina had noted on many occasions, of going through the motions of showing the respect due to her position—for she had most assuredly never told *him* not to bother with the formalities!—while apparently showing not a crumb of respect for her personally. Abominable man, she thought now, her skin prickling with antipathy.

There were a number of reasons why Caterina loathed Matthew Allenby. For a start, he was arrogant and too clever by half. He was a shameless social climber and he had too much influence over her brother.

An Englishman of unknown origins, for his background was swathed in mystery, he had come to San Rinaldo just under a year ago to advise on some building projects that the Duke was involved in. For, though still only in his mid-thirties, he was an internationally renowned architect, though Caterina had heard stories that he'd got where he was by ruthlessly sticking knives into the backs of his rivals.

At any rate, his association with the Duke had strengthened. Pretty soon, it seemed, he was spending far more time here, in the sunny little Mediterranean dukedom of San Rinaldo, than he spent in his own, more rainy homeland. But, though she detested all he was, this wouldn't normally have bothered Caterina, for her path and Matthew's very rarely crossed, in spite of the fact that, in addition to his town office, these days he also had an office at the palace.

No, the reason why she detested him was much more personal. For it was thanks to Matthew Allenby that, last September, she'd lost the love of someone who meant the world to her.

Thinking back on that time, she fixed him with a steely look as he turned with that maddeningly easy smile he could switch on and proceeded to address the still bewildered-looking Rosa.

'It must be about your lunchtime? Perhaps you wouldn't mind leaving us? Lady Caterina and I have things to discuss.'

'Of course, Mr Allenby. Right away.'

Caterina noted how the girl flushed with pleasure beneath his gaze as she switched off her computer and reached for her bag. Clearly she was one of those women who found him irresistible, who failed to see the viper beneath the good looks and potent charm.

Though it wasn't only women Matthew Allenby conned. Men, too, were taken in by that powerful aura of his. Even the normally astute Duke, for some inexplicable reason, failed to see him for the self-seeking hypocrite he was. Damiano treated him like a friend, when really he was no friend. He only courted the royal family to gain influence and social standing.

Caterina waited until Rosa had taken her leave of them, then she turned, with a frosty little smile to face him.

'You know, you really needn't have bothered getting rid of Rosa. I don't know what you think we could possibly have to discuss. I came to see my brother but, since he's not here, I shall simply come back and see him later.'

And so saying, she swung round and headed for the door.

'Suit yourself.'

Quite unperturbed, Matthew watched her departure. He had known she would react like this for he knew what she thought of him and, quite frankly, her antipathy didn't matter to him a damn. He let his eyes sweep unhurriedly over her willowy figure, dressed in a simple straight blue skirt and a matching round-necked top, as informal and casually elegant as her glossy light brown bob. She was so unassuming in some ways, so impossible in others, with a wild streak he sometimes thought it might be amusing to tame.

But, right now, they had other business on hand.

As she was about to disappear back out into the corridor, he observed to her back, 'You seem to be unaware that your brother has assigned me to deal with the problem you came to see him about. That's why I'm here. I understood it was urgent.'

'*You?*'

Stopping in her tracks, Caterina swung round to glare at him.

'*You?*' she ground out again. 'My brother assigned you? Well, maybe I don't want my problem dealt with by *you!*'

'Maybe you have no choice.'

'Oh?' Such arrogance! 'And says who?'

Matthew looked back at her without a flicker. 'Maybe that's just the way it is.'

Normally, Caterina's complexion was creamy and flawless, a perfect luminous foil for her china-blue eyes, which, most of the time, were filled with warmth and humour. But two angry red spots had risen to her cheeks now and her eyes were as warm and humorous as chips of ice. Even her soft-lipped mouth, which smiled and laughed so easily—though it had done its fair share of crying in recent months—was drawn into an uncharacteristic tight, angry line. Matthew really did have the worst possible effect on her.

She replied between her teeth, 'Well, I'm afraid it's *not* the way it is.' She would stick needles in her eyes before she would discuss her business with Matthew Allenby! And she turned sharply away to resume her interrupted exit.

But then Matthew spoke again. 'I think I should warn you that your brother has handed over the organisation of the garden party to me.'

As he paused, Caterina swung round again, just as he'd known she would. She glared at him, daggers flying from her eyes.

Quite unfazed, he continued, 'That's why I said you had no choice—for it was about some problem relating to the garden party that you wished to see your brother, I believe?'

He believed correctly, and it was intolerable that he should be aware of her business. Caterina said nothing for a moment, just glared at him furiously, wishing she had the power, simply with a look, to make him melt like a disagreeable blob into the carpet.

But there seemed little hope of that. All too physically substantial, he continued to stand there by the open doorway. Then, with a shrug, he observed, 'But maybe it wasn't important.' And, with that, apparently dismissing both her and her problem as of no further interest to him whatsoever, he proceeded to cross the room, right in front of her, heading for the door to the Duke's inner sanctum.

Damned impertinence! 'Where do you think you're going?' No one was allowed in there without her brother's permission!

Matthew totally ignored her admonition. Even as she stood there, bristling with indignation, he pushed the door open and disappeared inside.

Caterina was after him like a shot. 'Excuse me! If you don't mind...!' But in the open doorway she paused and blinked in disbelief. This was too much, surely, even for the monstrous Matthew Allenby?

He was standing by the huge carved mahogany desk that stood beneath a painting of Rino, the capital city, executed by the Italian master Canaletto during a visit to San Rinaldo in 1739. And he was picking up a pile of papers that lay there on the desk and riffling through them as bold as brass!

Not even Caterina would have had the nerve to do such a thing. No, not nerve. Nerve didn't come into it, she corrected herself swiftly. What this was was a case of barefaced insolence!

'Put those papers down at once!' She was hurtling towards him. 'How dare you? Nobody touches the Duke's private papers!'

He did not put them down. He did not even deign to look at her. He just continued, unperturbed, with his insolent riffling.

'Didn't you hear what I said?'

'Yes, I heard.'

And still he riffled.

'Then why don't you do as I tell you? Put those papers down this instant!'

She was standing right next to him, her eyes on his hands, which hadn't so much as paused in their insolent work, and suddenly she noticed something she'd never noticed before. He had exceedingly beautiful hands. Sinuous and very masculine, with long, dexterous fingers, sure and swift in their movements.

But what the devil was she doing admiring his hands? A little shocked at herself, Caterina flicked her eyes to his face, with its high, sculpted cheekbones and arrogantly curved nose.

'Mr Allenby, I'm warning you. Put those papers down at once!'

'I'll put them down, Lady Caterina, when I find what I'm looking for.'

Still he did not look at her. Still his fingers kept on searching.

It was too much for Caterina. 'I said put them down!' And she reached out angrily to snatch the papers from him.

'I wouldn't do that if I were you.'

Her hand never even made contact with the papers. Quick as a flash, Matthew caught her firmly by the wrist, his grip a band of steel pinning her to the spot, making something flare hotly and unexpectedly inside her.

'We don't want your brother's papers getting damaged, do we?' The iron-grey eyes pierced through her like bayonets. 'And let's get something straight.' His tone was as taut as a crossbow. 'I don't take orders from anyone, and very definitely not from you. I work for your brother. He hired me to do jobs for him. And you, I'm afraid, my dear Lady Caterina, don't enter into the picture at all.'

There was no trace of the famous Matthew Allenby charm now. What she was seeing was the real man, ruthless and dangerous, though this was only the civilised tip of the iceberg, of course. Caterina felt a shiver touch her spine at the thought of the dark savagery beneath.

Yet she did not back down. She tossed her glossy bobbed head at him. 'That's where you're wrong! I do enter into the picture! As his sister, I have a duty to protect the Duke's interests. You have no right to go rummaging through his private papers!'

'I'm sorry but I do. Every right, as it happens. Your brother asked me to pick up certain papers from his desk and that is precisely what I'm doing.'

He continued to hold her, his fingers cool around her wrist. 'So, you see, all your moral outrage is really quite misplaced.'

Was he telling the truth? Caterina suspected that he probably was. After all, she knew how thick he'd become with Damiano, exerting his evil influence all over the place—even on such unlikely matters as her love life, as she already knew to her painful cost. Yes, she decided reluctantly, he probably was in the right.

But only as regards her brother's papers. Regarding another small matter he had definitely overstepped the mark.

She narrowed her blue eyes at him and a little belatedly demanded, 'And now, if you don't mind, kindly let go of my arm!'

'My pleasure.' With an amused smile he released her instantly. 'Now,' he observed calmly, 'I can finish what I was doing.' And, turning away, he resumed his search through the papers.

Caterina watched him, hating him, though there was this much to be said for him—at least she knew exactly where she stood with him. For he clearly disliked her every bit as much as she disliked him. And, strangely, there was a perverse satisfaction to be had in the way they were able to clash so openly.

Still, they had never before clashed quite so openly as now—and certainly never with such unleashed physicality. Feeling that band of steel around her arm again, she shivered. Savage! she thought. How dared he lay a hand on her? The only reason why she hadn't demanded instantly that he release her was that she'd been so taken aback at the insolent black nerve of him.

'Here it is.' Matthew had found the document he'd been looking for. As he drew it out of the pile and laid the pile back on the desk, he cast her an amused look from the corner of his eye. 'Funnily enough,' he observed, 'this is a report concerning the garden party. The very event you wished to see me about.'

'Not you. My brother.'

'Ah, yes, your brother. Well, in this particular case, that amounts to the same thing. As I told you, he's put me in charge of the arrangements.'

'Congratulations. That's quite a coup.' Her tone was cutting. 'You'll be taking over his duties as head of state next.'

'I'm afraid I couldn't spare the time.' The gibe simply amused him. He held her eyes for a moment, enjoying her frustration—was there no way she could ruffle this wretched man's feathers? Then he continued, 'Your brother felt the garden party needed a new look this year. And I'm more than happy to take on the job.'

No doubt he was. The annual Montecrespi garden party, held each year in mid-July to celebrate the Duke's birthday, was one of the highlights of the European social calendar. Guests flocked from far and wide—from the United States, even Australia—for the honour of drinking vintage champagne and eating smoked salmon and truffles and wild strawberries, while at the same time rubbing shoulders with princes and earls, ambassadors and prime ministers and the cream of the entertainment world.

For as long as Caterina could remember, the transformation of the palace gardens into a suitable venue for this starry event—which had always been held in July, for the old Duke's birthday had been then too—had been left in the capable hands of Baron Igor. But the old man had recently died and someone was needed to fill his shoes. Caterina had been aware of this, but she certainly hadn't known that Matthew Allenby had been assigned to the job.

A sad thought struck her. In previous years she would have known. But these days she and Damiano were not so close any more—all thanks to the débâcle over her love life last September, a débâcle created by Matthew Allenby. And she found herself reflecting, not for the first time, that she would very much like to pay him back for that.

She told him now, disparagingly, 'Well, like I said, congratulations—though I must say I'm surprised you were given the job. I wouldn't have thought it was quite in your line.'

'No, it isn't, I suppose. It's not strictly architecture. But I quite enjoy getting involved in a bit of simple design from time to time. And it won't be too demanding. I'll be able to fit it in between other things.'

Of course. She had forgotten. This was Matthew Allenby, the human dynamo, who never had fewer than a score of projects running at any one time. In another man she would have admired the sheer energy and scope of him, but in Matthew Allenby it was simply one more aspect to despise. Especially since she knew—though of course he was unaware of this—that some of the projects in which he was involved were of a rather dubious legitimacy.

Oh, yes, she knew things about him he had no idea she knew!

'Well, that's all very interesting.' She smiled cuttingly as she said it, just in case he might delude himself that she actually meant it. 'However, you were wrong to assume that my problem concerning the garden party falls within your sphere of influence. You see, it was nothing to do with the design side of things that I wanted to speak to my brother about.'

She delivered him a cool look. He wasn't as omnipotent as he liked to think!

Or maybe he was. With a cool look of his own he informed her, 'I think you'll find that it probably does concern me. You see, it's not just the design side of things I've been put in charge of. Your brother has asked me to handle the whole lot.'

'The whole lot?'

'From top to bottom.'

Caterina narrowed her eyes at him. 'But surely not,' she insisted, 'including the guest list as well?'

'Yes, I'm afraid so.' He smiled at her look of horror. 'I've been put in charge of the guest list as well.'

But this was monstrous! Suddenly speechless, she blinked at him. The guest list to the annual Montecrespi garden party was virtually a sanctified roll of honour. There were some who would have sold their souls—and their mothers twice over—for the privilege of being on it!

The way it had always worked was that each member of the royal family submitted a list of proposed guests for the Duke's approval and Damiano then made the final decision. Handing over this responsibility to Matthew Allenby, number one crook and social climber, struck Caterina as being about as wise as setting a wolf to guard a chicken coop!

Though it did, of course, explain why she had a problem. And mentally she kicked herself. She ought to have guessed he was involved!

She glared at him. 'Well,' she said. 'I find this astonishing.' Then as he looked back at her impassively, quite unmoved by her astonishment, she put to him in a tight tone, 'Tell me something... The lists that were submitted by the rest of the family... were there any problems? Were their proposed guests approved or not?'

Matthew knew what she was leading up to, but he gave no hint of this as he replied, 'The Duchess's list was certainly approved without any problem.' He was referring to Sofia, Damiano's beautiful young wife, mother of the couple's eight-month-old son.

'And Leone's?'

Count Leone was Caterina's second brother, once known as an incorrigible playboy but now a happily married man.

Matthew nodded, still revealing nothing. 'I believe the Count's also went through without any problem.'

'Very interesting. And the Countess's?'

'No problem at all.'

'I see. So everyone else's went through without a hitch... Then how come,' she demanded, 'there was a problem with mine?'

Matthew regarded her for a moment. Then he told her in a flat tone, 'I'm afraid you included some rather unsuitable people.'

'Unsuitable in whose eyes?'

'In mine,' he responded. 'As I know they would also have been in your brother's.' And as he looked at her his eyes warned her not to pursue this subject further.

Caterina saw the warning and deliberately ignored it. 'Exactly in what way are they unsuitable?' she demanded.

'They had certain connections.' There was an edge of steel to his tone now. 'Certain connections which sadly rendered them quite unsuitable to be guests at a royal garden party.'

Liar! If anyone was unsuitable it was him! But these people who had been so peremptorily crossed off her list—as she had discovered only this morning, with the party just two weeks away—had been friends of Orazio, her ex-boyfriend. And that, as she well knew, was sufficient reason for Matthew's veto.

She thought of an old saying: my enemy's friend is my enemy. Well, Orazio had certainly been Matthew

Allenby's enemy, for he had dared to try and expose him for the two-faced scoundrel that he was. Little wonder then that Matthew, who had so much to hide, should prefer to keep his enemy's friends at a distance.

Caterina looked at him now, full of anger and loathing. Because he knew how to fight dirty and because he had the ear of Damiano, he had triumphed easily over Orazio, disgracing him and putting an end to his romance with Caterina and turning Caterina's life upside-down in the process.

Damn him! Suddenly she'd had enough of this unpleasant confrontation. In a cold voice she informed him, 'I intend to take this up with my brother. I shall have your judgement overturned and these people will be invited to the party.'

Matthew did not argue.

'That's entirely up to you.'

But as she looked into his eyes Caterina had a feeling that he was probably already plotting how best to thwart her. That prompted her to inform him, just to defy him further, 'I shall make a point of having a word with him this very evening. The sooner this is dealt with the better, I feel. Yes, I shall speak to him before I go off to the Bardi dinner.'

As she added that last bit she couldn't resist a smile. She had briefly forgotten about the Bardi dinner that was to be held in the Town Hall with herself as hostess this evening. A sumptuous affair, the purpose of the dinner was to celebrate the awarding of an important new contract to build an extension to the Bardi Home for Disabled Children, one of the many charities of which Caterina was patron. And the reason why she had smiled was that she knew something that Matthew

Allenby was unaware of. Something that would not please him in the slightest when he found out.

Feigning innocent curiosity, she tilted her head at him. 'Will you be attending the Bardi dinner?' she enquired. Though, knowing what she knew, she was pretty certain he would not.

Matthew, who did not know what she knew, nodded. 'I might.'

'And the presentation this afternoon?'

'Yes, I think that will be interesting. I shall definitely go along to that.'

Of course he would! He wouldn't miss it for the world! For Caterina happened to know that he had secretly entered the contest that had been held for the Bardi extension contract—secretly, for he had entered under the name of Tad UK, one of his lesser-known companies in London. And he would be there at the presentation this afternoon, when it would be Caterina's happy duty to announce the name of the winner, no doubt expecting, in his arrogance, that the winner would be him.

For the name of the winner had not been made public. Not even the winning company knew yet that it'd won—which was why all the contestants had been invited to attend the presentation, as well as the celebratory dinner this evening. And today's announcement of the winner was going to be a really big event.

It was also going to be a thoroughly demoralising one for Matthew Allenby, for though he thought himself incredibly clever he had come nowhere near winning. Caterina smiled at that thought. It was deeply cheering, as also was the fact that he would not be at the dinner. For she knew very well that a man of Matthew Allenby's towering self-importance was scarcely likely to want to show his face in defeat.

She threw him an oblique look now. 'Yes, it will definitely be interesting.' Then, out of sheer badness, savouring his imminent humiliation—for an architect of his standing didn't enter such a contest, even anonymously, unless he intended winning—she added, 'The winning design is really quite superb.'

He was watching her with a curious look. 'Of course, you know who the winner is.'

'Indeed I do. I was on the panel that did the choosing.'

And the rejecting, she thought with a twist of satisfaction, though she had rejected his design—as had the rest of the panel—not because it was his, for they had only discovered the connection later, but simply because it quite genuinely wasn't good enough. Still, when she had found out, it had given her an immense amount of pleasure.

Mock-innocently now, she added, just to stir him up a bit, 'It's a foreign company. One we'd never heard of. And, like I said, the design is really quite brilliant. It'll be my privilege to finally meet their representative this afternoon and present him or her with the contract for the extension.'

Matthew smiled a shuttered smile. 'You're making me curious,' he told her. 'I shall be watching the proceedings now with even more interest.'

Caterina smiled back at him sweetly. And I'll be watching you, she was thinking. And it will be my inestimable pleasure to see the look on your face when I stand up on the podium and announce the winner.

As she turned to go, there was a cheerful spring in her step. The day was turning out not so badly after all.

The atmosphere was electric as the seven members of the panel, with Caterina at their head, dressed in a butter-yellow dress, stepped out to loud applause onto the stage.

And as she looked out over the rows of faces—for the hall was packed to the gunnels—Caterina felt a fierce thrust of excitement and satisfaction. It had been hard work organising the contest, but it had been a resounding success. Entries had poured in from all over the globe and the publicity it had stimulated had done nothing but good for her beloved charity. Donations had more than trebled over the past six months.

And for a moment she quite forgot her private beef with Matthew Allenby. Since the break-up of her romance she had turned her back on men and love and poured all her energies into her charity work, and she was thrilled that this particular project had turned out so well.

All her charities were dear to her, but Bardi especially so, and she was deeply involved in the new extension. And now she couldn't wait to meet the winner of the competition, for it would be her duty and her privilege to work closely alongside him.

The panel members took their seats as Signor Roberto Lecori, chairman of the Bardi children's home, stepped up to the microphone to make an introductory speech. A hush fell across the hall and the audience settled back in their seats, all eyes fixed on him, as he began to speak.

All eyes, that was, except a pair in the fourth row which were fixed unblinkingly on Caterina.

She looked quite beautiful, Matthew thought. Serene and relaxed. Not at all the spiteful vixen who had confronted him a few hours earlier. His eyes narrowed; he was intrigued. There were so many different sides to her. Any man who got involved with her would have a real challenge on his hands. And he smiled, savouring that thought. He had always enjoyed a challenge. What a stroke of good fortune if fate were to throw them together.

He let his gaze sweep over her as he sat unseen in the fourth row—for he was aware that she hadn't spotted him yet—and the iron-grey eyes were full of appreciation. She really was quite stunning, far more beautiful than she seemed to realise, for she possessed none of the vanity that often accompanied such beauty. That wonderful glossy hair, that lovely face so full of character, that softly feminine, willowy figure...

Though not *too* willowy these days, as had been the case a few months ago at the time of the break-up of her romance. And as he remembered her unhappiness and how thin she'd got then Matthew felt a twist of regret at his part in the whole débâcle. Though, of course, he'd had no choice. He'd had to intervene. But he was pleased to see that she'd recovered. These days she was looking perfectly splendid.

And again he reflected that it really would be rather nice if fate were to offer him the opportunity to enjoy this gorgeous creature.

Signor Lecori was coming to the end of his speech now and the audience were starting to shift expectantly in their seats as the moment they had all been waiting for grew near. Then at last he turned to Caterina.

'And here to announce the winner... our beloved patron, the Lady Caterina...'

Caterina rose to her feet, smiling, though inwardly she was cursing. For the past ten minutes, with the utmost discretion, she'd been searching the sea of faces for a glimpse of Matthew Allenby. But there was no sign of him at all. Damn it, she was thinking. Was she to be denied, after all, the pleasure of looking into his face and seeing his disappointment when she announced the winner?

'Thank you, Signor Lecori...' She took her place on the podium and turned to address the audience before her. 'Ladies and gentlemen...' she began. But then her heart jumped inside her—for, joy of joys, at last she'd spotted her quarry!

He'd been half-hidden behind a woman in a wide-brimmed hat, but from up here on the podium she could see him perfectly—looking, it must be said, as dangerously handsome as ever in a dark blue suit and bright red tie. And as he met her eyes and smiled she mentally rubbed her hands with glee. In a couple of minutes' time he wouldn't be feeling much like smiling!

She began the short speech she had prepared, praising the high standard of the entries, her eyes flicking from time to time to the face in the fourth row, savouring the moment, fast approaching, when she would see the confident look in those dark grey eyes crumble.

And as the moment drew near her heart was hammering. It was shameful just how much she was going to enjoy this!

She paused. 'And now it's my very great pleasure to announce the winner, whose design, in spite of the high standard of its competitors, stood out, in the unanimous opinion of the judges, head and shoulders above the rest...'

Her gaze flicked to the fourth row. Here it comes, she silently warned him. Brace yourself for a nice big disappointment.

'And the winner is...' She licked her lips mentally. 'The winner is Secolo Designs of Geneva!'

The audience burst into applause, everyone looking excitedly round them to see who would stand up to claim the prize. But, before she did likewise, Caterina turned with a smile to focus for a gloating moment on the figure in the fourth row. That's one in the eye for you, Matthew Allenby! she thought.

But what on earth was happening? Her heart tripped inside her and suddenly her blood was turning to powder—for, right before her eyes, Matthew was rising from his seat and, with a triumphant little smile, walking towards her.

## CHAPTER TWO

'For a piece of blatant, barefaced dishonesty I would say that really takes the cake!'

The presentation was over, all the photographs had been taken and Caterina and Matthew were back at the Palazzo Verde, confronting one another across the desk in her private office.

At least Caterina, white with fury, was confronting Matthew, her hands tight fists as she glared at him across the desktop, wishing she could pluck his arrogant head from his shoulders, bury it at the bottom of some dark and spidery hole and never have to look at his hateful face again.

Matthew, for his part, was having no such violent fantasies. As he sat in the tan leather armchair opposite her he was feeling thoroughly pleased with the way things had turned out. And he was aware—though he really wasn't looking that way on purpose—that his air of quiet satisfaction was simply driving Caterina crazy.

'Dishonest?' he queried, not quite managing to suppress a smile. 'What on earth makes you come to that conclusion?'

'Secolo Designs of Geneva! That's what makes me come to it! That was a pretty shameless bluff!'

'Bluff? Why do you call it a bluff? It's the name of one of my companies.'

'Oh, yes! I know!' Her blue eyes sparked angrily. 'How clever, and how convenient for you to pull that out of the bag! Did you invent it specially for the occasion?'

It had been the shabbiest trick. Only someone like Matthew Allenby could have stooped so low as to pull a stunt like this. Caterina shuddered, remembering how her blood had turned to powder when she had read out the name of the winning company and seen Matthew rising to his feet.

Just for a moment she hadn't believed it. She'd blinked. Thought she must be dreaming. But no, there he'd been, mounting the steps up to the stage, coming towards her with a smug, triumphant smile to accept the contract for the Bardi extension. It hadn't been a dream, after all. It had been a waking nightmare!

After that, she'd had to endure the torture of a photo-call. She'd had to stand there shaking his hand before a battery of press photographers, a smile pinned to her face, going through the motions of pretending to be delighted that this perfectly monstrous man had just walked off with her precious contract.

It had been ghastly. Utterly ghastly. Her flesh had crawled just to think of it. And as soon as it was over she had taken him to one side and demanded that he see her in her office back at the palace immediately. Before this thing went any further, she wanted a few explanations.

Needless to say, he had kept her waiting. She'd been wearing out the carpet for at least fifteen minutes, pacing backwards and forwards, steam coming out of her ears, before he had deigned to poke his arrogant head round her office door.

'Sorry,' he'd offered, clearly not sorry in the slightest, 'but I got tied up with a bunch of reporters. They wanted to know how I felt about winning the contract.' He'd smiled into her black face. 'I told them I was over the moon.'

Caterina had known, of course, that he would enjoy rubbing her nose in it. For his triumph wasn't just triumph at winning the contract, it was also triumph at having so roundly trumped her. He knew how she felt about him and he was loving every sordid minute of this.

He said now in response to her accusation, 'It's not my fault you didn't know Secolo was one of my companies—and has been, as a matter of fact, for the past two years. You see, it wasn't just invented for the purpose of hoodwinking you.'

And from the slight edge of admonishment in his tone as he said that Caterina deduced that she was actually supposed to believe that he was totally incapable of such deceit. Hah! she thought scathingly. He must think I was born yesterday!

'If you'd done a bit of checking up,' he added, 'you could easily have found out.'

That had occurred to Caterina too, but there had been no cause to check up on the various contestants who'd entered designs for the competition. The designs, after all, had been judged solely on merit. Any additional information just hadn't been deemed necessary.

All the same, she observed now, bitterly, 'I very much wish I had checked up.'

'You mean you would have voted differently if you'd known?' He made a pretence of looking quite shocked at this notion. 'For someone with your high moral standards, surely that would have been unthinkable?'

Caterina eyed him. Let him mock her and make fun of her if he liked—they both knew that *he* didn't suffer from moral scruples!—but it did genuinely trouble her that when she'd asked herself certain questions earlier she hadn't been at all sure of her answers. Could she really have voted knowingly for Matthew Allenby? Could she posssibly have done otherwise given that his design was by far the best?

'I think,' she said, frowning, coming to a decision, 'that I would have had no choice but to resign from the panel of judges.' It sounded rather extreme, but what else could she have done?

'I see.'

Matthew seemed to contemplate her answer for a moment. Was he offended, Caterina wondered, to know the strength of her antipathy? With anyone else she would have avoided such callous bluntness. But not with Matthew Allenby. She didn't care if he was offended. And anyway, as she well knew, he could take it.

Which was one of the reasons why it was almost a pleasure to clash with him. When you were mad with Matthew Allenby you didn't have to hold back. You could just say what you were thinking and go straight for the jugular.

He continued to watch her in silence for a moment. Then he pointed out, 'But you didn't resign over the Tad UK entry... and I think you knew my connection with that company?'

Caterina could not deny it. 'Yes, I knew it was one of yours.' Then she looked at him and smiled. 'But there was no dilemma with that one. I wouldn't have voted for that design whoever's it had been.' And her smile turned unrepentantly malicious as she added,

'You must have been having an off-day when you did that one.'

'It wasn't that bad. It had one or two good features.' Then, seeing her expression turn openly disdainful at this apparent display of self-justification, Matthew smiled and informed her, 'I had no hand in it, however. It was the work of one of our new trainees. Not bad at all, I thought, for a beginner.'

Caterina was careful not to let her expression alter. So she was to be denied even the small pleasure of having thwarted him on that one! Damn, she was thinking. He was as slippery as an eel!

She leaned back in her chair and narrowed her eyes at him. He was totally maddening. Irritating beyond reason. What she really ought to do was wind up this meeting and spare herself the displeasure of another moment of his company. But she felt disinclined to do that. There was something about him. Something that seemed to stir in her a strange and fierce compulsion. The irritation and antipathy that he aroused in her was so acute, it was like an itch that simply had to be scratched.

And, besides, she hadn't finished with him yet. Not by a long shot.

She told him, her tone accusing, 'I really think you should have told me that you'd entered a design for the competition. Surely that's what any normal person would have done?'

Matthew eyed her and smiled. 'I had my reasons for keeping silent. After all, I wouldn't have wanted people accusing me of seeking favours by making my interest in the contest known. I am close to the Duke, after all, and you are his sister. People might have thought I was seeking special consideration.'

Yes, that was possible. People might have thought that. Though it hadn't even crossed Caterina's mind until this moment. For it was actually a totally ludicrous notion. Pigs would fly before she would give Matthew Allenby 'special consideration', and these days virtually *any* associate of her brother's would be liable to receive exceedingly short shrift from her. It was sad, but true. Their once close relationship really had sunk that low since the bust-up over Orazio.

She laughed a harsh laugh now. 'How little they know!'

'How little indeed.'

Matthew knew what she'd been thinking. At least, he knew she'd been thinking about Orazio. And, hearing that harsh laugh, it suddenly struck him that perhaps he'd been wrong when he'd made the assumption that she was completely over that sad affair. For at the heart of that laugh he had sensed real pain.

What she needed, he reflected, was a new affair to take her mind off it. And he wouldn't mind in the slightest providing the therapy himself.

Out loud he returned to the earlier point he'd been making. 'By making known my interest in the contest I would simply have been putting you in an uncomfortable position. And I would never have forgiven myself,' he added as though he really meant it, 'if you'd felt obliged to resign from the judging panel.'

Such kind consideration. He was making her heart weep. Caterina delivered him a look as cynical as his sentiments. 'I had no idea you possessed such an altruistic streak.'

'I tend to keep it well hidden. My modesty demands it.'

'Modesty as well?' Her eyebrows lifted.

He smiled. 'Naturally I try to keep that hidden as well.'

'Without too much difficulty, I imagine.' She flicked him a dry look. 'I must say this is really most revealing. All these fine qualities I would never have guessed at in a million years.'

'Really?' The dark eyes were fixed on her. 'How very ungenerous of you.'

'Not ungenerous, just realistic.'

She looked right back at him, at the arrogantly handsome face, so full of secrets, at the dark grey eyes with their menacing allure that, if you weren't careful, would suck you in and seduce you. He was many things—a cheat, a scoundrel and a social climber, as well as a dangerous male force to be reckoned with—but alas he was none of the fine things he was claiming.

'I judge what I see, and what I see,' she told him, 'rather contradicts those unlikely claims you're making.'

'Which only goes to show how deceptive appearances can be. But never mind,' he smiled. 'Once we're working together, you'll have plenty of opportunity to explore below the surface.'

Up until that point, though he'd irritated her beyond reason, Caterina had been quite enjoying their verbal fencing. So many of the men she encountered were so timid in her company, afraid to put a foot wrong, reluctant to contradict her. And she grew tired of it. At times it could be downright wearying being surrounded by people who agreed with you all the time.

And at least Matthew Allenby never did that. Even when he wasn't actually fighting with her he wasn't necessarily agreeing with her either. And, though she hated to admit that there might be anything she actually liked about him, she did in fact rather enjoy that side of him. Arguing with him gave her a buzz. A strictly intellectual buzz, of course!

But that last comment had definitely not been to her liking—that cool, breezy reference to their working together. For that was something she simply couldn't let happen.

Couldn't and wouldn't. She must find a way out of this dilemma. That was something she had realised very quickly. The Bardi extension was her pet project. She'd poured months of dedication and energy into it and she'd been looking forward to working alongside the winner and seeing the whole thing come to life. But there was no way she could work alongside Matthew Allenby, so a solution had to be found that somehow eased him out.

And in the course of the past hour or so two solutions had occurred to her—one quite civilised, the other rather more brutal. She would try the first one first and see if she could avoid spilling blood.

Speaking calmly and keeping her tone as matter-of-fact as she could manage, Caterina enquired, 'Do you really think we'll be working together?'

Matthew looked surprised. 'I had certainly assumed we would be. You're in charge of this project, aren't you? And I understood from the brief that you planned to be heavily involved in its execution.'

She shrugged. 'Yes, I do.'

'Then we'll be working together.' And he smiled a maddening smile, clearly relishing this prospect.

Caterina dropped her eyes, trying to gather her thoughts calmly. She must handle this with great delicacy or it would blow up in her face. One whiff of her true motives and he'd refuse to play ball.

She told him, 'The problem is you're a very busy man. I know you're involved in several projects just for my brother alone—including now,' she added with what she hoped was a benevolent smile, 'the organisation of the garden party. All these things take up time and, as you know, the Bardi extension's rather urgent... I fear it might be putting just a little too much pressure on you to expect you to work on it as well...'

Was she striking the right note? She tried to judge as he sat watching her, his long, supple frame leaning casually against the chair-back, the strong tanned fingers lightly clasping the arms, his eyes fixed on her face, an impenetrable smile on his lips.

He said, 'You're quite right. I do have a lot on my plate.'

Inwardly, Caterina sighed a small sigh of relief. Well, at least he hadn't instantly shot her down in flames. That mild response even suggested that she might be on the right track. She crossed her fingers mentally and carried on.

'You've already done the important part by producing the winning design... Its implementation...well, that requires less talent...and you have so many companies, so many talented people working for you...' She swallowed and finally spat out the conclusion she'd been working towards. 'I can't help feeling it would take the pressure off you if you were to appoint one of your employees to do the actual donkey work.'

Matthew watched her for a moment, saying nothing, seeming to give some thought to her proposal.

'That's certainly the way I sometimes do things,' he confessed.

'It makes sense.' Reassured, Caterina hurried on. 'I mean, you can't be expected to do everything yourself. That would just be crazy. After all, you're only human.' She forced a sympathetic smile. 'You can only stretch yourself so far. And this isn't such a terribly important project, after all. I'm sure you have far more important ones to claim your time. So it really would be more sensible to hand this one over to someone else.'

'I suppose there might be a kind of logic in that.'

As he nodded, Caterina congratulated herself. I've done it! she was thinking. And she smiled to herself, feeling a huge lift of elation.

'Well,' she said, relief pouring through her—for it looked as though she'd got her way without having to spill blood. 'I'm very glad we're in agreement about that.'

Matthew smiled a slow smile, holding her eyes with his own as he did so. 'You know...' he said, letting his gaze wash over her, touching her face, her neck, her shoulders, then moving down to the soft swell of her breasts in a way that was so unexpectedly yet so openly sensual that Caterina, totally thrown, found herself just sitting there, as though he had taken a hammer and nailed her to the chair.

'You know, when you calm down a bit, when you relax, when you smile, you really are quite extraordinarily attractive,' he told her. 'I was thinking that this afternoon, when you were on stage at the reception. You seemed totally relaxed and you looked quite beautiful.'

'Oh?'

Caterina forced the monosyllable between stiff lips. What she really wanted to do was tell him quite frankly that she had no wish to hear his opinion on such matters. But two things were stopping her, one she could control and one she could not.

The first was a reluctance to upset this sudden mellow mood of his. She had got what she wanted and she would be mad now to blow it just for the pleasure of putting him in his place.

But the second thing that was stopping her was the strangest sensation of somehow being mesmerised by the force of those dark eyes, a sensation somehow both pleasurable and quite intolerable at the same time. And it gripped her like a vice. She could not shake it off.

The grey eyes smiled. 'I hope you're going to be like this this evening. Then we can really enjoy our dinner together.'

Caterina blinked. She had almost forgotten about the dinner. She was expected to partner him, as winner of the contest, to the celebratory dinner at the Town Hall this evening. That fact flicked her back to reality, for she'd been dreading the dinner, and that feeling of being mesmerised abruptly vanished. Though she kept her expression sweet. She must not antagonise him. And, anyway, the prospect of dinner no longer seemed so ghastly. It would, after all, be the last unpleasant chore that she would be required to perform with him.

With a smile she put to him, 'Perhaps we can discuss at the dinner tonight who you might like to replace you on the job? You might even want to make an announcement to the other guests at some point?'

And she sat back in her seat. The whole thing was virtually sewn up.

But Matthew's expression had changed. 'An announcement?' he was saying. Then he shook his head. 'You've got it wrong, I'm afraid. There'll be no one replacing me. I intend to do the job myself.'

'But you said—' Suddenly Caterina was sitting up very stiffly in her seat. 'Wh-what do you mean?' she stuttered. 'You just said you would!'

'I said no such thing.' His expression had hardened again. 'All I said was that your suggestion contained a kind of logic. But it's always been my intention to see this project through personally.' He smiled a harsh smile. 'Sorry to disappoint you.'

So he had tricked her. Caterina glared at him, quite speechless for a moment. He had known all along why she was trying to edge him out—not out of concern for his heavy workload at all, but because she couldn't stand the prospect of working with him.

And he refused to play ball. Well, that was to be expected. But the matter wasn't settled yet, even though he seemed to think it was. She'd tried the soft approach first; now it was time to get tough.

She fixed him with a direct look. 'I think you're making a big mistake.'

'A mistake?'

'It wouldn't work.'

He feigned innocence. 'Why on earth not?'

'You really need to ask?' Caterina grimaced as she elaborated, 'We're not even capable of conducting a civil conversation. How on earth could we possibly contemplate working together?'

'It might be hard, I confess.' He smiled. 'Think of it as a challenge.'

Caterina did not smile back. 'There are challenges and challenges. And this one, I'm afraid, just doesn't appeal to me. No, you and I will not be working together.'

One dark eyebrow lifted. 'I'm sorry to hear that.' He regarded her narrowly for a moment then put to her, 'I take it this means *you'll* be handing over to someone else?'

'No, it doesn't mean that. This project is my baby. I wouldn't dream of handing it over to someone else.'

'In that case, you've lost me.' The dark eyes regarded her unblinkingly and it was impossible to tell what was going on in his head. 'If neither of us is planning to hand over to someone else, surely that means we'll be working together?'

'No, it doesn't. You see, whether you like it or not, you won't be doing the Bardi job.'

'Won't I?' His tone was low but had a definite edge to it. 'You're going to have to explain why. I'm afraid that makes no sense to me.'

As she faced him, Caterina's heart was thumping inside her. And now that the moment had come she found herself hesitating. It was harder than she'd thought, playing the heavy.

'Quite frankly,' she said, 'I'd hoped to avoid this sort of unpleasantness—'

'Unpleasantness?' He continued to watch her. 'What kind of unpleasantness are you talking about?'

Caterina swallowed hard. Damn and blast him, she was thinking. Why did he have to cross my path in the first place? But she couldn't back down now, even though what she had to do came far from naturally. She simply had to get him off the job.

She swallowed again. 'The sort of unpleasantness, I'm afraid, that could ruin your career and have you thrown out of San Rinaldo. You see,' she hurried on before her nerve deserted her, 'I know things about you... things you wouldn't want made public... and I'm prepared to use them against you unless you withdraw from this job.'

There, she had said it, and as she stopped speaking her blood was pounding. Breathing carefully, she watched him, waiting for his response.

She did not have long to wait. He began to rise to his feet. In a voice like sandpaper he said, 'So, that's what this is all about? Well, I think I've heard enough.' He flicked her a look as hard as granite. 'But you're wasting your time. I won't be withdrawing.'

'Oh, yes, you will. You'll have no choice in the matter once my brother gets to hear the things I know. And that's what I'm going to do. I'm going to tell him everything. Unless,' she stressed again, 'you drop out of the Bardi job. If you're prepared to do that, I won't say a thing.'

Matthew said nothing for a moment, then he fixed her with a stony look. 'Blackmail's an ugly thing, you know. It doesn't really suit you.' Then, as she looked away, fighting a blush—for he was right, this didn't suit her—he added in a tone grown suddenly heavy with contempt. 'No doubt this is one of the unsavoury little tricks you learned in the course of your association with Orazio?'

It was like a slap across the face. Caterina's sense of unease vanished. She looked back at him now, seeing only the hated face of the man who had been responsible, with his lies and his slanders, for all the emotional hurt she'd recently suffered.

Her heart filled with bitterness. Why should she feel uneasy about employing a bit of blackmail on a man like Matthew Allenby—a man who, in spite of the high moral tone he was taking, was far from being a stranger to such methods himself? Why, his hands were as black as the blackest corners of his soul!

She told him, her tone cutting, 'No, I didn't learn it from Orazio. I'm simply using the sorts of tactics that I feel sure you're familiar with.'

'Well, they won't work, I'm afraid. Face facts. You're a novice.' The dark eyes flayed her. 'I'm way out of your league.'

Quite possibly he was, but he was still not as invulnerable as he believed. As he started to turn away, she angrily informed his back, 'I'm not bluffing, you know. I know all about you. And I have evidence in my possession. Real, tangible evidence. I shall expose you for the cheat and the charlatan that you are.'

Matthew was almost at the door when she finished the sentence. Unhurriedly, he turned round and looked into her face and his eyes were a pair of steel hooks tearing into her.

'You know,' he informed her, 'you're making a big mistake. I'm really not the best man to pick a fight with. People who pick fights with me invariably end up regretting it. And I guarantee,' he added in a tone like a whiplash, 'that you will be no exception to the rule.'

Never before had Caterina seen such a look in a man's eyes. A look without mercy. Black and menacing. But instead of feeling scared, or outraged, or angry, what she felt was a sudden flare of reckless excitement and a trickle of anticipation like cool fingers down her spine. She was going to thoroughly enjoy the fight ahead.

Matthew continued to watch her, then, with a quick, cynical smile, he inclined his head briefly in his usual parody of a salute.

'Goodbye for now, Lady Caterina. Until dinner this evening.'

Then he turned and strode swiftly from the room.

There was only one thing for it after that encounter with Matthew Allenby—a nice long bubble bath laced with oil of patchouli to help restore her frayed and tattered nerves.

'Help!' she'd told Anna, her personal maid, when she'd returned to her private quarters still seething with anger. 'Be an angel and run a bath for me. I think I'm going to explode!'

And that was where she was now, up to her chin in scented bubbles, listening to Anna happily singing to herself next door as she got Caterina's things ready for the dinner this evening. Though she was only listening with half an ear. Most of her attention was focused on trying to sort out the hopeless jumble in her head. Her brain felt as though it had been attacked by an electric blender.

Damn Matthew Allenby! Damn him to infinity! What had she ever done to deserve this blight on her life?

She lay back, letting her hair trail in the water, and gazed up at the painted and gilded ceiling with its pictures of water nymphs and seashells and dolphins. In a way, she felt appalled by the stance she'd been forced to take with him, threatening to ruin him and have him kicked out of San Rinaldo. She must have sounded like some heavy in a second-rate gangster movie! But what alternative did she have? She simply could not work with him. And anyway, after what he'd done to her, he deserved every nasty thing she could fling at him.

She sighed. In the beginning, of course, she hadn't realised he was such a viper. She'd known little about him, other than that he worked for her brother, and their paths had crossed only on brief and rare occasions so that the two of them had remained virtual strangers. He had really only become of interest to her when Orazio had opened her eyes.

Orazio. Her gaze still fixed on one of the water nymphs, she paused in her thoughts and let her mind settle on Orazio.

She had thought she was in love with him, but now she suspected she never had been. She had got over him far too quickly for it to have been love. But she had been fond of him. He had been fun and a decent and caring person, and he definitely hadn't deserved to be treated as he had been.

The whole disaster had happened, of course, because of what he knew about Matthew Allenby. For he had a friend, he had told her, who had once worked for Matthew and who had told him all about the way he went about his business. Bribes, intimidation, secret handouts, blackmail. These were the methods by which he had got where he was. And, of course, by the careful courting of those with influence and power.

'Your brother can't possibly realise what kind of man he's got tied up with. For God's sake warn him,' Orazio had advised her just a short while after they'd started seeing each other.

And she had. She'd gone to Damiano and told him everything and her brother's response had been very clear and simple. 'Accusations without proof are worthless,' he'd told her. 'Show me some evidence and then we can start talking.'

And so Orazio had set about gathering together what they needed—files and letters and tapes and photographs—and they had planned that, as soon as he'd gathered enough, Caterina would present the whole lot to Damiano. She'd gone along with this plan not out of any malice towards Matthew Allenby, for at that stage she'd had nothing personal against him, but because she loved and wanted to protect her brother.

But neither she nor Orazio had realised they were playing with dynamite.

The first hint of the shambles that lay ahead had been when Damiano, who didn't normally interfere in her private life, had started expressing disapproval of Orazio—not saying anything specific, just that he considered him unsuitable—and brother and sister had exchanged sharp words on the subject. But Caterina had not been prepared for the avalanche that was to follow.

It had happened quite out of the blue. Damiano had called her to his office and proceeded to regale her with a list of accusations against Orazio.

'He's a crook,' he'd told her, 'a two-bit crook and a lowlife, and I can't allow you to continue to see him.'

Caterina had been outraged. She'd refused to listen. How dared he make these false accusations?

'I know the real reason!' she'd stormed at him. 'It's because he's a commoner! Well, I won't stop seeing him and you can't make me!' Then she'd added, just out of bravado, because she was so damned mad at him, for really there had been no such intention in her head, 'I might even marry him if I decide it suits me!'

That had been when Damiano had, almost literally, exploded. 'Take my word for it,' he'd warned her, 'that that will never happen!' And there and then he had ordered her to break off the romance immediately or he would cut her off without a penny.

He'd meant it, too. But that hadn't stopped Caterina, as she'd swung out of his office in tears of helpless rage, retorting defiantly, 'I don't care! I won't stop seeing him!'

For she could be as hard-headed as Damiano and, besides, it was a matter of principle. She would not be dictated to in this fashion.

And she would have stuck to her guns if Orazio hadn't talked her out of it and insisted on making a discreet withdrawal.

'I can't let you make this sacrifice,' he'd told her. 'I'd never be able to live with myself if I did.'

Besides, he'd no longer had a job nor much hope of finding another one. Word was already being circulated that he was *persona non grata*—Damiano hadn't wasted any time there—and it really hadn't looked as though there was much of a future for him in San Rinaldo. So within a week he'd been gone, in spite of Caterina's pleas that he stay on and at least fight to redeem his good name. 'I'd rather sacrifice my good name than bring you embarrassment,' he'd told her. And that had been the end of the romance.

It was only later, through various bits of palace gossip that had trickled down to her, that Caterina had become acquainted with all the murky facts. Damiano had not acted because Orazio was a commoner—something that had become clear to her a short time later when he had given permission to their brother Leone to marry an American girl. No, his disapproval of Orazio had had another cause entirely.

And it could be spelt out in five syllables. Matthew Allenby.

For it had been Matthew who had fed the stories to Damiano that had caused him to become convinced that Caterina's lover was a crook—stories that had now also reached Orazio's former business associates and besmirched his name in San Rinaldo for ever. And it was easy enough to guess what had prompted Matthew's actions. He must have discovered what she and Orazio were planning and had decided, in typical fashion, to stick the knife in first.

Caterina sighed now and sank back amongst the scented bubbles. At that point she'd tried to get hold of Matthew so that she could force him to retract all the lies he'd told Damiano. It was too late to save her romance, but the record ought to be set straight. But her plan had come to nothing, for Matthew had disappeared off to the States, and by the time he had returned, just over a month later, her feelings regarding the whole incident had altered.

She still smarted at the way Orazio had been taken from her and she was still mad at Matthew for blackening her lover's name. But she was not distraught at her loss. What really distressed her was the rift that had opened up between herself and her brother.

Though he was twelve years older, she and Damiano had always been close. He had been her friend and her confidant as well as her brother. But that closeness was all gone now, had been replaced by anger and silence, for she just couldn't forgive him for the way he had treated her.

And she missed him. A precious chunk had been torn from her life. Like a constant throbbing pain she felt the lack of it. And this was the real tragedy that had broken her heart six months ago and for which she would never forgive Matthew Allenby.

Countless times she'd dreamed of paying him back. She'd thought of all the evidence Orazio had gathered and which he'd left in the safe-keeping of his sister, and she'd pondered on how she could use it against him.

But she'd done nothing, of course. Pursuing a vendetta was not in keeping with her character. And as to using the evidence for the purpose that had been intended, namely to draw Damiano's attention to the nature of the viper he was involved with... well, she no longer felt inclined to do her brother any favours. If he wished to befriend vipers, then be it on his own head.

For her own part, she had decided that the simplest and best strategy was just to act as though the Englishman did not exist—though on the few occasions when they'd met it had been her pleasure to cross swords with him. About anything and everything. About nothing at all. She would simply make a point of contradicting whatever he said and generally being as disagreeable as she possibly could.

But she had never brought up the subject of the Orazio fiasco with him. In fact, she'd avoided that subject with great care. There was no saying what she might end up doing to him if they got on to that.

Things would probably have remained in this state of controlled hostility if the business about the Bardi extension hadn't cropped up. But now... well, now the situation was different. Now something simply had to be done.

'M'lady!'

There was a call from the other side of the bathroom door.

Caterina sat up, poking her head out of the bubbles. 'Yes, Anna? What is it?' she called back.

'M'lady, you asked me to keep an eye on the time. It's just gone seven. Shall I call down for the hairdresser now?'

'Thanks, Anna. You're a gem. Tell him I'll be ready for him in ten minutes.'

Caterina was smiling now. That little think session had cleared her brain and her earlier qualms had all melted away. She would do what she must do to nail Matthew Allenby and, what was more, she'd make her first move at the dinner this evening.

That thought made her feel good. She rose slowly from the bubbles, the warm, scented water streaming like liquid pearls from her body as she reached for one of the blue towels piled on the shelf at her back. And as she paused for a moment before wrapping it round her she was really quite as beautiful as the gilded water nymphs on the ceiling, with her slim, feminine figure and high, rose-tipped breasts that would surely have tempted any man with red blood in his veins— though no thought could have been further from her mind at that moment.

No, she was thinking of Matthew Allenby. What was it he'd said? That she'd end up regretting picking a fight with him? Well, they'd see about that! He'd discover he'd underestimated her. At the end of this fight *he'd* be the one with regrets!

And as she stepped from the bath she felt, just like before, that thrust of excitement deep inside her and the trickle of sweet anticipation like cool fingers down her spine.

## CHAPTER THREE

'WELCOME, Mr Allenby! Come and join us! Let me introduce you to some people I don't think you've met.'

As Matthew, dressed in an immaculately cut DJ, appeared in the foyer of the grand Rino Town Hall, which was already packed with glittering VIPs, Caterina stepped forward with a dazzling smile to greet him. And no one amongst that distinguished gathering looking on could have suspected just how hard she was having to grit her teeth.

Matthew knew, of course. And he knew something else as well, something which was betrayed by the sharp, direct look behind her smile. She had decided not to heed his warning of this afternoon. Though that was not a surprise. It was what he had expected. Well, fine, he thought now. He enjoyed a good fight. Especially with an adversary as beautiful as she was.

He returned her smile. 'Good evening, Lady Caterina.' And he treated her to one of his deferential little nods that somehow managed not to be deferential at all. Then as their eyes met and held, the blue ones flinty, the grey amused, he suspected that this was going to be a thoroughly entertaining evening.

It was certainly going to be a grand one. The Rino Town Hall, even on a normal day, was a pretty impressive sort of place. It had been built in the eighteenth century as the home of a wealthy nobleman and the elegant sweeping staircase, high vaulted ceilings and wonderful frescos that adorned the ancient walls still bore testimony to its lofty pedigree. But tonight it was glittering even more gloriously than usual—thanks in part, it must be said, to the assembled company, who between them were wearing enough diamonds to light up the night.

Caterina, dressed in a perfectly stunning aquamarine ballgown that lent her eyes a depth of blueness as intense as a summer sky, was wearing a couple of her favourite diamonds too—a necklace that had belonged to her beloved late mother and a pair of earrings she'd been given on her twenty-first birthday. They were delicate pieces. Quite exquisite, but not showy. And though she wasn't particularly addicted to wearing diamonds—she felt more at ease on the whole when dressed casually—she always very much enjoyed wearing these.

And besides, it was expected of her. It was her duty to dress up. When a member of the ruling Montecrespi family appeared at an illustrious gathering such as this one people expected a bit of glitter and glamour for their money!

That aside, though, Caterina was actually rather grateful to be dressed up to the nines this evening. In her diamonds and Versace ballgown, being fêted and fawned over—an inevitable consequence of being the sister of the Duke—she was feeling, as she always did on these occasions, a little like an actress playing a part. It was a feeling she normally hated, but not this evening. For it would simply make it easier for her to put on a show with Matthew Allenby. The role she had to play with him would just be another part of the act.

For tonight she must pretend to be his gracious companion. All smiles and rapt attention and flattering glances. There must be no harsh words, no angry exchanges. And the ugly business of her ultimatum must not be mentioned. Quite simply, it was her duty to look as though she was having a wonderful time.

So far, she was playing her part superbly.

'Let me introduce you to Signor Gherardi, our Lord Mayor,' she told Matthew as she proceeded to lead him down a line of local dignitaries, flicking him a quick, knowing glance as she did so. For this, as they both knew, was what he was into—mingling with the rich and powerful and the various social luminaries who could assist his rise up the social ladder. And, though no one else guessed, she knew that he understood perfectly the total contempt in which she held him.

'And here's someone I'm sure you're very keen to meet,' she observed *sotto voce* before continuing in her normal voice, 'Count Riccardo, the man who owns that wonderful castle just outside Rino.'

'Count Riccardo and I have already met.' With one of his charming smiles, Matthew shook the man's hand. 'The Count and I share a special interest in sailing. In fact,' he added, as though deliberately for Caterina's benefit, 'I had the pleasure recently of spending a most enjoyable weekend on his yacht.'

A special interest in sailing! What a perfect pastime for a social climber! He really knew, Caterina reflected, how to pick his hobbies! He probably also enjoyed a bit of polo!

In fact, it was perfectly clear that he knew his way around pretty well. Caterina soon discovered that he was already acquainted with quite a few of the local bigwigs.

'I see you haven't been dragging your heels when it comes to making the right connections,' she commented drily once the introductions were over and they were standing together, waiting for the signal to head into the main assembly room where the dinner was to be held.

'I've made a few tentative forays.' Matthew cast an amused smile across at her. It really didn't bother him when she made these sorts of comments. 'But nothing to compare with the strides I've made this evening. The last half-hour with you has been worth its weight in gold.'

'So glad to have been of service.' Her tone was pure irony. 'No doubt you'll now be getting to work on them all, buttering them all up, collecting more invitations for weekends on yachts.'

'What an excellent idea.' He ignored her irony. 'You're quite right—one mustn't let the grass grow under one's feet.' Then, as the assembly-room doors opened and they were about to start moving, he paused and looked at her. 'Aren't we forgetting something?' He held out his arm to her for her to slip hers through. 'Nothing personal, you understand, but I believe it's procedure.'

He was right, of course. Caterina flicked him a sideways look as, reluctantly, she slipped her arm through his, trying hard not to be conscious of the muscular, virile warmth of him. To distract herself she observed scathingly, 'I see you know your social etiquette.'

'One has to,' he smiled back at her. 'A familiarity with social etiquette is an absolute essential for any social climber.'

They were proceeding at the head of the line of guests and dignitaries into a room that, to anyone not accustomed to such a spectacle, was guaranteed quite simply to take your breath away. Chandeliers twice the size of Count Riccardo's yacht blazed like vast torches from the gilded ceiling, magnificent paintings hung from the walls and the entire splendid tableau was reflected endlessly in the vast Venetian mirrors at each end of the room.

And though Caterina, probably more than anyone in that august gathering, was used to moving in exquisite surroundings—for the Palazzo Verde was one of the finest royal residences in Europe—even she let her gaze drift appreciatively round for a moment. Anyone, she was thinking, would have to be impressed by such beauty. Except Matthew, of course. For one of the tricks of being a successful social climber was to pretend that you'd seen it all before.

They'd reached their places at the top table and he was standing aside while one of the liveried footmen pulled out her seat for her. Once she was seated, he allowed the man to do the same for him.

He never put a foot wrong, Caterina thought with irritation. He never fumbled or looked awkward. He did it all with impeccable elegance, as though it was forged into his brain and he'd been doing it all his life. What a phoney he was!

She turned to him with a smile, as though making polite conversation. 'You really do know how to dot your i's and cross your t's. You clearly take this etiquette thing extremely seriously.'

'Extremely.' He smiled back at her. 'I did a correspondence course, in case you're wondering, and most invaluable it proved to be, too. Part one told you the correct way to hold your fork and knife and not to pick your nose in public. And by the time you'd arrived at the more advanced chapters you were learning all sorts of rarefied gems, like how to have dinner in the company of a royal lady without disgracing yourself by spilling vichyssoise down the front of your hired suit.'

He was pulling her leg, of course. The dark eyes danced with devilment. But Caterina refused to be amused by his humour.

She smiled a disdainful smile. 'One has to admire your tenacity.' Though her tone made it clear that she admired nothing about him. 'You really are astonishingly devoted to your goal.'

'That's the only way to reach your goal—by being totally devoted to it. I very much believe in strength of purpose.'

Caterina had no trouble at all accepting that claim. One look into his face and you could see that strength of purpose—in his eyes, in the way he looked at you, in the ruthless set of his mouth. Whatever he set his sights on, in the end, would be his.

She felt a flicker of ambivalence now as she looked at him. Normally, that was a quality she would have greatly admired, for she respected that kind of drive, that fearless kind of energy—but only when it was harnessed to an honest and worthwhile goal, which in Matthew Allenby's case it most assuredly was not. And suddenly it struck her that that was really a little sad.

He was watching her in that amused, slightly detached way he had, and suddenly Caterina found herself curious. 'So, tell me,' she put to him, 'what is this goal exactly that you're so single-mindedly headed towards?' She knew in general terms, of course—he was after influence and position—but it might be interesting to hear it from the horse's mouth, as it were.

The grey eyes flicked a smile at her. 'Are you talking long-term or short-term? If long-term, I must admit my goals are pretty extensive. But if you're talking strictly short-term...' he sat back in his chair a little and allowed his gaze to drift over her face '...I would say that my principal goal at this moment is simply to enjoy an evening in the company of a beautiful young woman.'

'How kind.'

It came out sounding less ironical than she'd intended, for, foolishly, she'd felt the strangest tingle as he'd looked at her. She'd never noticed before the extraordinary beauty of his eyes—for the predominantly dark grey colour was flecked with amber and green, lending them a wickedly sensual quality. They were the sort of eyes, she found herself thinking, that could easily melt a girl's resolve.

She felt a shaft of horror. Where had that thought come from? Pushing it hastily away, she added in a scornful tone, 'How sweet of you to pay me such a charming compliment.'

Matthew smiled with amusement. 'I mean it,' he told her. 'You really are looking quite ravishing tonight.'

'Oh, really? That must be because I'm feeling so relaxed.' She held his eye as she made this cynical allusion to his observation of that afternoon. 'No doubt the effect of your wonderfully soothing company.'

'You think so?'

As he continued to watch her, he had one hand propped lightly on the table-edge, and for some reason Caterina found herself glancing down at it. She had a thing about hands. Men's hands, that was. And Matthew's were a very fine example, as she'd already noticed earlier today. Strong and masculine, sinuous and well shaped.

She felt another shaft of horror and snatched her gaze away. What the devil was wrong with her? First his eyes, now his hands. Was she going soft in the head?

She pulled herself together. 'So, what about these long-term goals of yours? You said they're pretty extensive. Do you want to tell me what they are?'

'All of them?'

'The most important ones. I'm curious,' she smiled. The smile was part of her act, of course, but she was a little curious.

Matthew leaned back in his seat and smiled a light smile. 'I want to be the best architect in Europe, for a start...'

'Only in Europe?'

'You think I should aim higher?'

'Well, aren't you the best architect in Europe already?'

'How nice of you to say so.' He totally ignored the heavy irony. 'But I really think you flatter me. I'm not the best yet.'

'Ah, yes, of course.' She continued to smile at him. 'I was forgetting about that famous modesty of yours.' Then she narrowed her china-blue eyes and demanded, 'So, apart from being the best architect in Europe, what other goals do you have on your list?'

Matthew continued to watch her. She's quite lovely, he was thinking. Even lovelier than I'd realised. Even more enchanting.

It truly was going to be a pleasure getting to know her better—something he intended, with increasing determination, to do. For over the past half-hour or so in her company an idea had been taking shape in his head.

He told her, 'Of course, one day, I'd like to get married.'

Now this was interesting. 'To a nice little countess?'

'She needn't be a countess.'

'Then what about a count's daughter?' Caterina paused and pointedly held his eyes. Everyone knew about his relationship with Claire, glamorous younger daughter of Comte Jean de Pliey. Caterina had never actually met her but she'd seen plenty of photographs. 'Does this mean a marriage to the lovely Claire might be on the cards?'

Even as she said it Caterina was a little surprised at herself. It really wasn't done to ask such personal questions. But as soon as it was said she felt a little safer, nicely distanced from those hands and eyes she'd been admiring. Besides, with Matthew it was different. There were no rules with Matthew. Whatever she said, he wouldn't bat an eyelid.

He didn't. 'I can't honestly say I've really thought about it,' he said.

She was sure to believe that! A man like Matthew Allenby would give his right arm to marry into the French aristocracy! But you really had to hand it to him. He knew how to play it cool.

Caterina continued to watch him. 'I must say,' she put to him, 'that I'm a little surprised Claire is not here with you tonight.'

Again, he did not bat an eyelid. 'Are you?' was all he said.

'Yes, I am. After all, the dinner invitations were addressed to the contestants and their partners.' And Claire had been his partner for nearly a year now. 'I would have thought you would have wanted to have her here with you.'

'I'm sure you're right, but alas she was otherwise engaged.'

His tone was light, without the faintest hint of regret, and as Caterina looked back at him she found herself reflecting that what she had always supposed was more than likely true. His relationship with the glamorous French aristocrat was more a tool in his quest for social advancement than anything remotely to do with love. And he didn't need her here tonight. She had no real purpose to serve.

She felt a stab of disapproval. What a charlatan he was. People weren't people to him. They were just convenient stepping-stones.

He was saying now, 'Anyway, it makes a very pleasant change to enjoy the company of a duke's sister instead of that of a count's daughter. And I'm sure I can equally rely on you to keep me in line should I happen to forget my social etiquette. If I start disgracing myself by eating my peas off my knife, you will be sure to tell me, I hope?'

'Oh, I'm sure there'll be no need.' Caterina did not smile back. 'I'm sure you've studied your etiquette handbook most meticulously—with the same single-mindedness that you do everything else.'

Then she added, just out of malice, for his shamelessness really maddened her, 'It must be quite a strain never being able to relax, always having to work so hard at making the right impression.'

'You think so?' One black eyebrow lifted in amusement. 'You think I might be happier eating my peas off my knife?'

'That might be pushing it a bit. But maybe you could try just being yourself.'

'You mean truer to my origins?'

'Yes, truer to your origins.' As she looked into his face, Caterina felt a flicker of curiosity. For, of course, she had no idea what his origins actually were.

No one seemed to know. In the infrequent articles about him in the Press—infrequent, for he tended to keep a very low profile, which was hardly surprising given some of the things he was up to!—no mention was ever made of his family background. Even Orazio hadn't known exactly where he had sprung from.

'I've heard various stories,' he'd once told Caterina. 'That he's the son of a jailbird. That his father was a teacher. That he never knew his father. That he was brought up by some maiden aunt. Whatever the truth is he's taken great pains to cover it up, so I suspect his origins are probably every bit as unsavoury as he is.'

Maybe, Caterina had decided, unsure what she believed herself. The only thing that could be ruled as certain was that Matthew Allenby was a man of mystery, his past and much of his present shrouded in enigma, a man hidden behind a whole armoury of dark secrets. And it would be intriguing to peel some of that mystery away, to discover what really lay behind the amber- and green-flecked eyes.

No, it wouldn't! she hurriedly corrected herself, snatching her gaze away. She had no interest whatsoever in knowing anything about him. She despised him and all she wanted was just to get him out of her hair!

It was as though he had read her mind and now took pleasure in crossing her.

'You know,' he said, smiling, 'I'm really glad I won your contest.' As the waiter appeared behind them and poured champagne into their glasses, he raised his in a toast. 'Here's to us,' he proposed. 'May this partnership of ours lead to great things.'

Caterina joined in the toast only because people might be watching, but he really was in for a disappointment, she was thinking. There would be no partnership. There would be no great things. All there would be was him out on his arrogant ear.

She smiled to herself. And towards this highly desirable end she would be making her first, crucial move after dinner.

But first the dinner...

There were seven courses in all, each one more astonishing than the one before it—caviare, fresh salmon, pheasant, truffles—the whole thing a towering culinary triumph. Indeed, the guests were all so impressed that the entire team of chefs—on loan for the evening from the Palazzo Verde—were brought in from the kitchen to receive a round of applause. This was definitely an evening that wouldn't be forgotten in a hurry.

Caterina, like everyone else, enjoyed the meal immensely. And not just the meal. To her total amazement, she also thoroughly enjoyed Matthew's company.

At first, she tried to keep their exchanges to a minimum. There were limits, after all, to her acting abilities and too much of Matthew, she feared, might lead to indigestion. So she turned her attentions to the other guests instead. But that didn't work out, and for one simple reason: Matthew quickly established himself as the focal point of the table. Pretty soon, all eyes and ears were on him.

And no wonder. He was a quite brilliant and amusing raconteur, with a typically laid-back English sense of humour that clearly delighted his fellow guests. It delighted Caterina, too. She had rarely been so entertained.

She sat back in her chair and watched him through lowered lids. He had such poise, such easy self-assurance, and enough charm to sink a whole fleet of ocean liners. Though there was nothing remotely bland about him. There was always that edge, that spark of mystery that flashed and tantalised at the back of his eyes. And he was just so heart-achingly good to look at. Watching him was intoxicating, like drinking vintage champagne.

And she was drinking him in greedily, scarcely aware of what she was doing. It was only as something warm and secret flared inside her that she lowered her eyes abruptly to the crisp white tablecloth.

She kept them there and gave herself a good brisk talking-to. Was she out of her head? Had she had too much to drink? This was Matthew Allenby, number one snake and all-round bad guy. He might look pretty good, but he was rotten to the core.

Feeling a little more safely distanced, she glanced up cautiously and fixed him with a carefully critical blue gaze. That really was a first-class correspondence course he'd taken, or maybe he'd invested in private lessons on how to charm dinner guests!

When the meal was finally over, coffee served and brandy poured, all the speeches applauded and all the toasts drunk, some of the guests left their tables to mingle a bit. And this was the moment, Caterina decided, for her to make the move she'd been planning. There were two people down at the bottom table she was rather keen to have a word with.

Excusing herself briefly, she rose from her seat, leaving the others and Matthew in conversation. Then she made her way between the tables, pausing to exchange a word of greeting here and there, as she headed for the middle-aged man with the moustache and his wife.

'Carla. Antonio. Good evening,' she greeted them. Then, 'No, don't get up,' she insisted firmly as, suddenly catching sight of her, they were about to leap to their feet. 'I just came over for a quick word and to say I hope you enjoyed the dinner.'

'It was a marvellous dinner, thanks.' Carla beamed at her plumply. 'We really enjoyed it. Didn't we, Antonio?'

'It was first-class. First-class.' Antonio stroked his moustache. 'Definitely the best dinner we've ever been to.'

Caterina smiled. 'I reckon my brother's going to have to give the chefs a raise. After tonight there'll be quite a few people after them.'

There was a vacant seat next to Carla. She sat down on the edge of it. 'Actually,' she continued, 'there's something I wanted to ask you. This isn't really the moment to go into explanations, but could I possibly come round and see you some evening? Tomorrow perhaps? Would that be convenient?'

'Of course, Lady Caterina.' Carla had turned quite pink with pleasure at the prospect of a visit from a member of the royal family. 'Tomorrow evening would be fine with us.'

'That's marvellous. Thanks. I'll try to be there around eight.' Caterina leaned towards them and began to add in a semi-whisper, 'It's about certain items that Orazio left in your care. I . . .'

But her voice trailed off as something quite extraordinary happened.

A tall dark man had appeared at Caterina's elbow and was taking her by the arm and drawing her from her seat. 'Excuse us,' he was saying, with a glance at Carla and Antonio, and in a tone as smooth as honey and as cold as polished marble. 'I'm afraid Lady Caterina's presence is required elsewhere now.'

Caterina had to suppress a gasp of mortal outrage. She also somehow managed, by an astonishing feat of self-control, to stop herself from snatching her arm free of her kidnapper and rounding on him with a furiously clenched fist. She had no choice but to control herself in such a public situation, as Matthew, of course, was perfectly aware as he proceeded to lead her away from the table.

She just had time to murmur to Carla and Antonio, smiling as she did so, trying to pretend that she was going willingly, 'Yes, do please excuse me. I'm afraid I've got to go.'

Behind the smile she was fulminating with fury.

Matthew led her into a quiet corner, behind an embroidered Chinese screen, mercifully out of sight of the other guests. And, as he released her at last,

Caterina rounded on him, outraged, her cheeks crimson with anger, her blue eyes blazing.

'What the hell do you think you're doing? Have you taken leave of your senses? Kindly explain what the devil's going on!'

If she had expected him to look contrite or even mildly apologetic she was in for a fairly hefty disappointment. For he was looking as mad as she was, his dark eyes flinty as he countered, '*I'm* the one who should be asking what's going on! What the hell were you doing with those people?'

For a moment Caterina was utterly speechless as they stood facing one another beneath a large oil painting of the courtship of Dionysus and Ariadne which really could not have been more out of keeping. Then she drew herself up tall and faced him squarely, this outrageous, detestable, arrogant man who had just subjected her to the most humiliating experience of her life—though she knew very well that he had done it most discreetly and that probably very few people had noticed anything out of the ordinary.

'Who the devil do you think you are?' she demanded hotly. 'How dare you behave like some damned caveman with me?'

Matthew was not remotely impressed by her outrage. He continued to glower down at her, eyes like black splinters, and, ignoring her question, repeated his own.

'What were you doing with those people?'

'I was speaking to them. They happen to be friends.' She spat the words at him like tin-tacks. 'Not that that's any damned business of yours!'

'You call those people friends?'

'Yes, I do. I call them friends.'

'Well, they didn't look to me like the sort of people you should be calling friends.'

'Is that a fact?' What staggering arrogance! 'And what makes you think I'm the least bit interested in your opinion?'

'I'm sure you're not, but you'll listen to it anyway. Those people are definitely not suitable to be called friends.'

'And what is that supposed to mean? Is this some kind of middle-class snobbery?' Typical, she was thinking, of the *arriviste* that he was. 'Shouldn't I consider them friends just because they're ordinary people? Well, unlike you, I don't choose my friends according to their class.'

'That's exceedingly worthy of you. But, worthiness aside, I would say you rather lack discrimination. You see, I happen to know who those people are.'

Caterina faltered for a moment. She hadn't realised that. Then she tilted her head at him in a gesture of defiance. Well, so what? She had no reason to hide the truth.

'So, you know who they are? Well, it's no great secret, anyway. They're Orazio's sister Carla and her husband.' She fixed him with a direct look. 'And it's none of your damned business if I choose to go and have a word with them.'

'Maybe you're right, but I'm making it my business anyway.' He paused. 'Who invited them here? Was it you?'

'What's this? The third degree?'

'Just answer the question. Did you invite them to the dinner?' And he took a step towards her as though he might grab hold of her again.

Having no wish to be grabbed, Caterina took a step back. 'Yes, I did, as a matter of fact!' Though she hadn't, of course. She'd simply heard that they'd be coming. 'And what of it?' she challenged him. 'How dare you interfere? Haven't you interfered enough in my life already?'

Emotion flashed across her eyes. Hateful man and his interfering! Look what had happened to her last time he'd gone sticking his nose in! She had ended up losing the precious friendship of her brother!

Matthew caught that flash of emotion but totally misinterpreted it. So he'd been right, he was thinking. She wasn't completely over Orazio. And he felt a stab of irritation. This was going to make things more difficult for him.

He said, 'Take my word for it, these people are no good for you. Put them behind you. They belong to a chapter that's over. Don't try to hang onto what's best let go.'

Caterina looked at him and instantly understood something. He believed she was still emotionally attached to Orazio. And she very nearly laughed. That was utterly ridiculous! But she stopped herself in time. It would be better to let him think it. Let him believe she'd been fixing a tryst with her ex-lover when really what she'd been doing was making an appointment to go and pick up the damning evidence against him that Orazio had left in the safe-keeping of his sister!

She smiled to herself, enjoying her secret. Soon, very soon now, she would pay him back for what he'd done to her. She was still smiling when he turned smartly on his heel and walked away.

\* \* \*

Caterina was feeling thoughtful as her chauffeur drove her back to the palace that evening just a little after midnight. And it was with a distracted 'Goodnight', not her usual cheerful smile, that she climbed from the black Mercedes and made her way up to her private quarters.

Her rooms were quite deserted, for Anna had long since gone to bed, though she had turned down the sheets on Caterina's big four-poster and left the bedside lamps switched on, just as she always did. And though usually Caterina appreciated these thoughtful little touches, tonight she barely even noticed them as she kicked off her shoes and slipped out of her blue dress.

She stretched and yawned. There was a lot to think about. It had been a funny sort of evening. Pleasing and enjoyable, in spite of that confrontation with Matthew at the end and the perfectly disgraceful way he'd behaved. She shuddered again, remembering how he had grabbed hold of her. Never in her life before had any man taken liberties like that!

It had been a satisfying evening too. The appointment she'd made for tomorrow evening meant that the proof she needed would soon be in her hands, finally putting her in a position to seal Matthew's fate.

She washed quickly and climbed in between the silk sheets, sinking back against the pillows. It was convenient that Matthew had jumped to the conclusion that she was still emotionally attached to Orazio. It meant that he was unlikely to suspect what she was really up to—especially since she'd told him that she already had the evidence in her possession!—and wouldn't be tempted to stick his interfering nose in for once!

Of course, he'd probably tell Damiano of his suspicions about her and Orazio, but that wouldn't matter because she'd be speaking to Damiano herself soon, sorting out everything from Matthew Allenby's demise to the garden-party invitations he'd had the insolence to interfere with. For she'd decided to confront Damiano with everything in one major session, at the end of which Matthew Allenby would be swept away in small pieces!

She stared for a moment at the blue silk canopy above her head, suddenly recalling how she'd almost laughed out loud when she'd twigged Matthew's suspicion that she was still in love with Orazio. Perhaps that seemed a little cruel, for she and Orazio had been close once, but the truth was that she'd felt nothing for him for a very long time.

She knew the reason why. It had been the way he had left her so easily, claiming it was for her sake, though she'd wanted him to stay and fight. That had wounded her deeply. It had also disillusioned and disappointed her. It was the real reason why she'd turned her back on men and love for a while. They simply weren't worth the effort, she'd decided.

But not all men were Orazios. She leaned back against the pillows. Some men had a bit more steel in them than that. And all at once an image of Matthew popped unsummoned into her head.

Those dark grey eyes with their arrogant gaze. That air he had of total self-assurance. Matthew, you could count on it, wouldn't have just walked away. He'd have stayed and he'd have fought them. He'd have thrown everything he had at them, in that typically single-minded way he did everything. And, in the end, he would have won.

She sighed, finding this image immensely pleasing. How wonderful to have a man like Matthew fight for you!

In the same instant she blinked, perfectly appalled at herself. Had she taken leave of her senses again? She detested the man!

Abruptly, she reached out and switched off the bedside lamps, as though she might extinguish at the same time the shameful image in her brain. But it refused to be extinguished. As she curled up beneath the sheet, eyes closed tight, fiercely willing herself to sleep, it simply wrapped itself around her, as seductive as a kiss.

## CHAPTER FOUR

WHEN Matthew got home that night there were three messages on his answering machine.

One was from the Duke, asking to see him at nine the following morning. The other two were from Claire, demanding with increasing hysteria that he call her immediately at her Paris apartment.

He glanced at his watch, however, and decided against that. It was too late for the sort of discussion he would inevitably have to endure, and besides, he wasn't in the mood after the events of the past evening, which had left his mind very much filled with thoughts of Caterina.

New thoughts. Exciting thoughts. Thoughts he rather wanted to concentrate on. For tonight at the dinner he had made a decision, adding yet another goal to that list Caterina had been so interested in, and right now he was finding it hard to think of anything else. So, no, he had decided, he would call Claire tomorrow morning.

But there was no reply when he rang her from his office at the palace just after he arrived there at eight-thirty. So he would have to phone her later, after his appointment with the Duke, about which he was feeling slightly curious, though he had a pretty shrewd idea of what it would be about.

The Duke was waiting for him in his private office, seated at his desk beneath the priceless Canaletto, and virtually the first thing he said, after a brief, 'Good morning,' was, 'So what's this I hear about Caterina? She's been making contact with these people again?'

So he had been right, Matthew thought. Damiano wished to speak about his sister. He nodded. 'Yes, I'm afraid she has.'

Matthew seated himself casually in one of the leather-backed chairs that stood in a semicircle facing the Duke's desk. He was dressed in a blue suit that looked every inch what it was—a superior example of Savile Row tailoring. The tan shoes on his feet came, naturally, from Lobbs, his shirt from Jermyn Street, his silk tie from Hermes. Though it had to be said that all this sartorial perfection was carried off with an air of total unselfconsciousness. Anyone looking at him would have assumed that he knew no other standard of dress.

That was if they even noticed the details of his dress, for it was actually rather likely that they would not. What struck one first and foremost about Matthew Allenby was not his attire but the sheer force of his personality. The hand-tailored London suit and the expensive French tie somehow failed to register in any great detail.

No, it was the essence of the man, not his appearance that impressed. And, besides, one couldn't help sensing that however he might be dressed, even were he to present himself in a T-shirt and a pair of old Levis, the effect would not be even marginally diminished.

That was also why, had it not been for the fact that Damiano was seated behind the desk, anyone observing the current scene would have been hard pressed to guess which of the two men was the Duke. In every way each appeared to be the equal of the other, and not least in the way they related to one another. There was no formality at all. They simply appeared to be friends. The Duke, a handsome, commanding-looking man, continued now as he sat back in his chair regarding Matthew through black-as-coal eyes, 'What do you think she's up to? Do you think she's starting up that damned affair again?'

Matthew felt a dart inside him. This was indeed what he feared. But he kept his tone neutral, concealing his personal feelings, as he answered, 'I wouldn't entirely rule that out.'

'Damned fool.' Damiano scowled. 'When will she ever learn?' Then his dark expression lightened. 'I was glad you intervened.'

Matthew shrugged. 'It was an impulse. I just felt angry when I saw her speaking to them.' He was aware of choosing his words carefully as he continued, 'Whatever her reasons, it can do her no good to get mixed up with them again.'

'No good at all.' Damiano's expression grew dark again. 'Neither personally nor as a member of the royal household—something I have already made abundantly clear to her.' And there was iron in his voice as he added, 'I will not have the Montecrespi name tarnished by being brought into association with those people.'

He glanced at Matthew and demanded, 'Do you think she got the message or is she likely to persist in this folly?'

'I couldn't really be sure. Let's just say I'm not too hopeful.'

Matthew was conscious that he was not being very forthcoming, and there were two very simple reasons for that. The first was that he disliked discussing Caterina with her brother. In the past he'd got involved because he'd really had no choice. Anyone in his situation, he reckoned, would have done the same. But he had not the least desire to discuss her private life or to speculate on what she might or might not be up to.

It was not that he in any way lacked sympathy for Damiano over the problem of his wayward sister. His feelings on the subject were very close to the Duke's. But last night he had acted very much on a personal impulse, not because the Duke would have wished it, and it rather irritated him that the incident had been reported back to the palace. Personally, he would never have mentioned it.

The other reason for his reticence was rather different. For the fact was that he had another theory about what Caterina might be up to, one that he preferred to keep to himself. She had claimed, regarding this evidence that she planned to use against him, that she already had it in her possession, but though that might, of course, be true Matthew was not convinced that it was. And he suspected that there might be some link between this evidence and Orazio's sister.

If that was the case, he preferred to keep Damiano in the dark and deal with the whole nasty can of worms himself.

Damiano understood at least one reason for Matthew's reticence. He smiled now and told him, 'OK, no more questions. You're my consultant architect, not my spy, I appreciate that. It's just that this damned situation bothers me.' Then he proceeded to change the subject, smiling mischievously as he observed, 'So, you've won the Bardi contract?

Congratulations. How do you think you're going to enjoy working with my sister?'

Matthew smiled back at him. 'A challenge. Definitely a challenge.'

He might have added that it was a challenge he intended turning into a personal triumph. For working with Caterina would provide him with the perfect opportunity for a great deal more than the casual dalliance he'd initially had in mind. It would allow him to realise the plan he'd committed himself to last night.

But he kept that to himself as he elaborated with a smile, 'I'm afraid I'm the last person she wanted on this job.'

'So she's still got it in for you? Silly girl.' Damiano smiled at him. 'Never mind, I'm sure that once she gets to know you she'll see how wrong she's been and revise her opinion.'

'Let's hope so.' Though Matthew was privately wondering as he said it just how well Caterina would ever know him. For there were certain things he intended keeping well hidden.

After that the conversation turned to more neutral subjects, namely the various architectural projects Matthew was involved in with Damiano, and in particular the Duke's plans for the construction in Rino of an international arts and crafts centre. It was almost lunchtime when Matthew got back to his office in the city centre where he normally spent his afternoons.

His secretary glanced up with a smile as he walked through the door. 'Good morning Mr Allenby,' she greeted him.

'Good morning, Julia. Everything run smoothly while I was away?'

Not that he actually had any doubts. The lovely Dutch Julia, fluent in five languages, was a positive paragon of efficiency—as she proceeded to prove now as she reeled off half a dozen messages, including one from Lady Caterina's secretary confirming that her ladyship would be dropping round about three.

Matthew hadn't forgotten. 'Excellent,' he nodded. He was very much looking forward to seeing the lovely Caterina again.

But then, as he was about to disappear into his private office, Julia added a piece of information that made his smile drop away.

'Mademoiselle Claire phoned as well. Several times, actually. I told her you'd get back to her as soon as you could.'

'Right. I'll phone her now.'

Matthew hid his irritation as he stepped into his office and crossed to the phone. But his fingers were stiff and angry as he punched in the number and they drummed angrily on the desktop as he waited for it to ring.

There was no reply, not even her answering machine. Matthew laid down the phone with a frown between his brows and stared with narrowed eyes into space for a moment. This whole Claire affair was starting to become a major headache. Somehow, and soon, he would have to sort it out. It was essential that he be free now to concentrate on Caterina.

Caterina had decided that her only option for the moment was just to grin and bear what fate had dumped on her head.

Well, bear, at least. Grinning might be a little harder. Though at least her suffering would be brief, she consoled herself. Tonight she would pick up the vital evidence, then she would go straight to Damiano and dump it on his desk. And that would be the end of Matthew Allenby!

In the meantime, however, there was a bit of purgatory to be endured, beginning this afternoon at three.

There was really no way Caterina could have got out of today's meeting. It had been part of the arrangement with the winner of the contest that they would meet for a couple of hours on the day after the presentation to discuss how the project could best be put into action. And since she had other appointments in town anyway today it made sense for her to go to Matthew's office rather than have him come to the palace.

She arrived at three on the dot, dressed in a cool blue linen dress and in a thoroughly businesslike frame of mind. She was not going to let Matthew Allenby upset her.

As Julia led her to the inner office, and before the girl could announce her, Caterina, taking the initiative, stepped boldly over the threshold.

'Good afternoon, Mr Allenby,' she announced.

And then she faltered and frowned. For he wasn't seated behind his desk.

Matthew had been standing by the window looking at some slides, but he turned round now to face her with an amused smile on his lips.

'And good afternoon to you, Lady Caterina,' he replied. 'I must say you're looking as lovely as ever today.'

Caterina felt like cursing him, partly for the compliment, which he probably didn't mean and wasn't required anyway, and partly for the way that, without even trying, he had managed to take the edge off her rather grand entrance. But though she started to scowl something very strange happened as she looked into his face and met the iron-grey gaze.

This was the face that had filled her thoughts as she had lain in bed last night after the dinner. This was the man she had felt thrilled to imagine as her champion. Her champion and her lover. Her very special lover. And no wonder, she thought now. He was the most attractive man she'd ever met.

As he watched her, Matthew could sense the essence of her reaction, and, it had to be said, it greatly pleased him. This boded well for his plans. Though he was under no illusions. He knew he still had a long way to go yet. But never mind; there was no hurry and he would get there eventually and it would be well worth the effort when he did.

He stepped towards her, pausing briefly to toss the transparencies onto his desk. 'A job I finished a few months ago,' he revealed with a glance at them. 'It's always interesting to see how a project looks through the camera's eye when it's finished.'

Caterina had just about managed to pull herself together and was now rationalising away those dangerous thoughts she'd been having. She'd been caught off guard, that was all. And as for last night... Well, she'd been tired last night. Those foolish fantasies didn't count.

She cast him an oblique look. 'And are you pleased with it?' she asked him. Though naturally he'd be pleased with it. He was pleased with everything he did.

'It'll do.' He smiled at her. 'At least, the client seems satisfied, so I guess that's something to feel pleased about.'

'Yes, I expect it is.'

His coolness was maddening, especially since her own earlier businesslike frame of mind appeared to have sprouted wings and flown out the window. Something kept flickering inside her each time she looked into his face.

'I expect you're very good at satisfying your clients,' she added.

Oh, dear. As soon as it was out Caterina felt like dying. That just had to be the mother of all Freudian slips! She glared at him, daring him to make some smart remark.

Matthew met her eyes and smiled. 'I do my best,' he answered. Then, seeing her embarrassment, he quickly added in a more serious tone, 'It's no good if I'm pleased with a project and the client isn't.'

That response, Caterina knew, deserved her gratitude. He had treated her slip-up with the perfect grace of a true gentleman. But she felt no gratitude. Perversely, she felt angry. He was so damned in control and she was all over the place!

Feigning a look of disbelief, she put to him in a mocking tone, 'Surely that sort of failure isn't something you've ever experienced?'

'It's never happened as far as I'm aware and I sincerely hope it never does.' He shrugged. 'But in these matters one can take nothing for granted.'

Caterina raised a surprised eyebrow. My, this was unexpected! He was actually admitting he wasn't perfect, after all! But she wasn't looking for things to agree with; she was looking to put him in his place.

She observed with a malicious little smile, 'Quite so, Mr Allenby. So I'd advise you to make sure that you brief your substitute most carefully. We wouldn't want him mucking up the Bardi job on your behalf.'

Ah. That felt better. Instantly it was back to battle stations and all those strange, dangerous feelings she'd been feeling had disappeared.

Matthew was frowning. 'Substitute?' he was saying. 'What substitute are you referring to, Lady Caterina?'

'You know very well what substitute I'm referring to. I've already told you I have no intention of working with you and I've warned you what I shall do if you try to insist...' She'd been about to elaborate in more detail, but her voice trailed off. She still didn't feel at all comfortable spouting threats.

But he had understood anyway. He nodded. 'Ah, yes. You plan to blacken my name and have me thrown out of the country—a scenario, I must confess, that doesn't appeal in the least.'

He stood and looked at her for a moment, a strange smile on his lips. Then suddenly he stepped back. 'Why don't you take a seat?' He waved to a group of bold-striped armchairs that faced the desk. 'Then we can discuss this little problem in more comfort.'

'There's really nothing to discuss. I've made my position quite clear.' But all the same she seated herself in one of the armchairs, noticing as she did so the wonderful view from the window over the higgledy-piggledy red-tiled roofs of Rino, with just a glimpse of the sunlit blue bay beyond. And she found herself saying, 'That's a pretty spectacular view. It must be one of the best views from any office in the centre.'

As she spoke she cast a quick glance round the office itself. It wasn't particularly large, but it was beautifully done up, with pale panelled walls decorated with architectural drawings and one or two rather excellent watercolours.

'This is a very nice place you've got yourself,' she added. 'It must be one of the most sought-after offices in Rino.' Then she fixed him with an intent look and added meaningfully, 'What a shame it would be if you had to give it all up.'

'It would be a terrible shame.'

Surprising her a little, Matthew had seated himself in the armchair opposite her rather than behind the big oak desk. He leaned back against the cushions now and regarded her closely as he continued, 'Especially since I've just spent a great deal of money having the studio upstairs enlarged. You see, I rather like it here. I'm in no hurry to go.'

He stretched his long legs out in front of him, crossing his elegantly shod feet at the ankles. Then he said, as though it were part of the same conversation and not a total *non sequitur* at all, 'I think it would be a good idea if we dropped the formalities. You call me Matthew and I'll call you Caterina. I don't know about you but I really would prefer it.'

Caterina was a little taken aback. The truth of the matter was that she had never been one to insist on formalities. All her colleagues at her various charities simply called her Caterina. But with Matthew Allenby it was different. She preferred to keep him at a distance. Not in terms of rank. Rank didn't come into it. There was just something deeply reassuring about having a barrier between them.

But she could hardly tell him that. It would sound most peculiar. So she shrugged. 'If you like. It makes no difference to me.'

Though, of course, she would never call him Matthew, she was thinking. That would be just a little too chummy for comfort.

'Good.' He nodded. Then he watched her for a moment. 'You know,' he said at last, 'regarding that demand of yours... that I hand over the Bardi job to one of my employees...' He smiled. 'That's not something that can be arranged overnight.'

Caterina was momentarily dumbstruck. Did this mean he was in agreement? She felt a rush of surprised relief. She wouldn't have to play the heavy after all! He must have thought it over and decided she was serious in her threats and that it just wasn't worth risking going against her.

She felt a lovely sense of triumph. Her strategy had worked! He was backing down!

Carefully hiding her feelings, she looked across at him. 'So, how long would you need to organise it?' she asked him. For there was truth in what he said and she should be generous in victory.

He laced his fingers together thoughtfully and rested his chin lightly on top of them. 'A week,' he said. 'That's the fastest I could do it. I'm going to London in a couple of days. I could set it all up while I'm there.'

A week sounded a bit long, but if he was going away anyway it wasn't so bad. Caterina regarded him. 'When will you be back? When can you have it all set up?'

'I'll be back for the Duke's birthday party. I could possibly bring a replacement with me or have him follow me here soon afterwards.'

Caterina was doing some calculations and what he was suggesting sounded acceptable. Damiano's birthday party—the private celebration that preceded the more public garden party—was due to be held in just over a week's time. Somehow she would force herself to wait until then.

She felt a weight slip away from her, though she was cautious as she answered. 'OK. We'll do it like that. But don't try anything funny. I was absolutely serious about those threats I made before.'

He smiled at her. 'Of course you were. Definitely no funny business. I promise you.'

They spent the next hour or so discussing the plans for the extension, working out a schedule for meeting builders and decorators and all the various people who would be involved in getting the thing going. And it was a satisfying sixty minutes in which they accomplished a great deal, principally because Matthew had already done much of the groundwork. One thing you had to say for him—he was a professional to his fingertips.

'OK. That's enough for now.' At last he sat back in his chair, tossing the papers they'd been studying onto the low wooden coffee-table that he'd pulled between them to use as a desk. 'Before we have a final check over these figures, I don't know about you but I need a coffee.'

'That sounds a good idea.' Caterina sat back in her seat too. All the talking they'd been doing had made her thirsty.

Matthew was rising to his feet. 'I'll nip down to the bar downstairs. Julia's off on an errand and I think we're out of coffee anyway. You wait here,' he told her. 'I won't be a minute.'

Caterina watched him as he disappeared, feeling oddly mellow. The past hour had been stimulating and she was almost feeling sorry that they wouldn't, after all, be working together. For he was a joy to work with. He knew his job inside out and he had a wonderful ability to communicate his knowledge and enthusiasm. Working with him would undoubtedly have been a valuable experience. And more than just valuable. It would have been exciting.

He had this ability to charge her up, and not only in a negative way. He seemed to tap some secret energy in her, to get the adrenalin going. He made her feel more alive than she had ever felt before.

It was as she was acknowledging this, almost wistfully, that the phone on his desk began to ring.

Caterina hesitated for only a moment. Then she crossed to the desk and picked it up. It might be important and, if it was, she could take a message.

'Hello? Matthew Allenby's office,' she said.

Next moment she was wishing she had just let it ring. Something jolted inside her as an imperious female voice with a sexy French accent demanded, 'Monsieur Allenby, please.'

It was Claire, of course. And Caterina was reacting most strangely. Suddenly, she felt as stiff as a plank of wood.

'I'm sorry,' she responded, at least sounding normal. 'Mr Allenby's not here right now. Would you like to leave a message?'

'Not there? Where is he?' There was a note of distress now in the voice.

'He's just popped out on an errand, but he'll be back in a minute. Shall I get him to call you back?'

'Yes, tell him to call Claire.'

And with that the line went dead.

Matthew walked back into the office carrying two paper cups of espresso virtually the instant she put down the phone.

Caterina glanced at him, suddenly feeling peculiarly on edge, her earlier mellow mood now totally departed. 'I just answered a phone call from your girlfriend Claire,' she told him. And she peered into his face to see his reaction.

There was no reaction to speak of, only the faintest lifting of one dark eyebrow. Matthew handed her one of the coffee-cups. 'Oh? And what did she have to say?'

'She wants you to call her back. That was all she said.' And it was total madness, but her heart was suddenly beating very fast.

'OK.' Matthew seemed to be hardly listening. He sat down in his chair again and took a mouthful of his coffee as he picked up the papers he'd tossed down on the coffee-table earlier. 'Thanks for taking the message,' he said.

Caterina continued to watch him, inexplicably pleased by his response and aware that it was precisely the response she'd been hoping for, although she hadn't actually realised she'd been hoping for anything. But his totally uncaring attitude rather confirmed the impression she'd got last night at the Bardi dinner. He wasn't in love with Claire. Nothing could be plainer. And, though last night she'd been scandalised by this revelation, all she was feeling right now was a sense of pure relief.

Which was shocking, she told herself, feeling a thrust of guilt and shame. And quickly, to ease these guilty feelings, she said, 'She sounded a little upset. Perhaps you ought to phone back right away. If you want privacy, I don't mind leaving the room.'

'I'll phone later.' He glanced up at her. 'Why don't you come and sit down again?' Then he added with a shuttered look as still she did not move, 'I'm sure it was nothing that can't wait.'

That look made Caterina wonder if he was feeling guilty too. Which simply made her feel worse, almost as though she had entered into some conspiracy with him against the hapless, unloved Claire. And suddenly she felt the need to distance herself from him, and to distance herself too from her own strange and shocking feelings.

She said, 'I don't think you're treating Claire very kindly. She wasn't at the dinner last night and now you're not phoning her back. That's not a very nice way to treat a girlfriend.'

Matthew was watching her with an expression that was impossible to fathom. For several seconds he said nothing, then he told her in a flat tone, 'If you want to check these figures with me you'd better sit down. If not, I'll do them myself after you've gone.'

That was a plain enough rebuke. Caterina blushed to her hair roots. It was quite clear that he considered Claire to be none of her business and, of course, he was absolutely right—she wasn't. Feeling about two inches high, Caterina went and sat down again in her armchair.

They worked together for another quarter of an hour or so, though Caterina's heart was no longer in it. She longed to wind up their meeting and get off to her next appointment. What an absolute fool she'd made of herself.

Matthew, as it happened, was feeling not a great deal more comfortable. He'd been surprised by her accusations, but he would gladly have answered them if only the answers could have been straightforward and simple. But nothing concerning Claire was simple these days and it had been his total frustration with the situation that had caused him to issue that rebuke to Caterina.

Which he regretted, for he could see that he had wounded her. And it really was not in his interests to do that.

At last they'd finished and Caterina rose to her feet gratefully. At that precise moment the phone rang again.

It was Julia, who in the meantime had returned from her errand. 'Mademoiselle Claire's on the other line. Shall I put you through,' she asked Matthew, 'or would you prefer to call her back?'

Matthew sighed. 'I'll call her back. Tell her I'll call back in five minutes.' And with a frown he laid the receiver down and stood staring at it for a couple of seconds.

Then he turned slowly to Caterina, who was carefully not watching him, a studiedly blank look pinned to her face. In a flat tone he said, 'Perhaps I ought to tell you something. Claire's no longer my girlfriend. I think you should know that.'

He didn't say why she should know that and Caterina didn't ask. In fact she couldn't have even if she'd wanted to, for she was having trouble just breathing. Suddenly her heart was jumping about like a ping-pong ball in her chest.

Matthew had come to stand in front of her as she still stood there, face averted. And now, very gently, he was reaching out towards her, catching her chin in cool fingers and twisting it round slowly so that although she still wasn't looking at him at least she was facing him.

'We all make mistakes in relationships,' he was telling her. 'It's simply our nature. We wouldn't be human if we didn't.' He paused. 'But the important thing is that we recognise our mistakes, cut loose in time and move on to better things.'

Caterina was looking at him now, her heart clattering inside her. At that barely veiled reference to her and Orazio her eyes had darted to his and she'd been about to rebuke him, but the rebuke had been stifled by the look in his eyes. Warm and seductive. Turning her insides to honey.

Then he said, 'I hope that's something you agree with?'

'I'm not sure.' Quite frankly, she wasn't sure of anything. She swallowed hard and said, 'I think I ought to be going.'

'OK. I'll see you out.'

And he seemed about to move away. But at the last minute he didn't. Instead, he bent and kissed her.

It was the briefest of kisses. His lips barely brushed hers. But never had Caterina experienced anything more powerful. From her scalp to her toes she seemed to light up like a light bulb. Her hair was standing on end. She was six feet off the ground.

'Until soon,' she heard him say. 'Very soon, I hope.'

Caterina was vaguely aware of nodding, then of being led through the outer office. And she dimly recalled saying goodbye to Julia, then shaking hands with Matthew outside the lift.

But it was perfectly possible that none of that happened. For it was at least another hour before she started breathing normally again and her feet finally re-established contact with the ground.

Well, that was just about the most disgraceful display of weakness I ever witnessed in my entire life!

For the hundredth time since it had happened a horrified Caterina was chastising herself, this time as her chauffeur drove her back to the palace. How had she ever allowed such a monstrous thing to happen? Matthew must have bewitched her. There was no other explanation.

But that that kiss had happened was really the least of it. More shocking was the fact that she couldn't stop thinking about it. Running it over in her mind. Reliving the giddy thrill of it. It was disgraceful, it was shameless, but she was quite out of control.

And that wasn't all. What was even more alarming was the way she kept going over what Matthew had told her about Claire. That she was no longer his girlfriend. Meaning, of course, that he was free. And the way that knowing that filled her with a giddy excitement. Hopes and dreams. Yes, she really was that mad.

Mad! she told herself fiercely. Mad, mad, mad! And she had to do something. She had to get a grip. She had to nip this dangerous madness in the bud.

But salvation was at hand. In less than an hour she would be on her way to see Carla and Antonio. And as soon as she had the evidence she would take it straight to Damiano, in spite of having given Matthew a week to step aside. He didn't deserve such consideration. He was far too dangerous. And she dared not risk a single day more in his company. A kiss today, she thought, shuddering, and—good lord—tomorrow what?

And she clenched her fists tight. Roll on eight o'clock!

An hour later, however, Caterina's plans were in disarray.

When she got to the house there was no Carla and Antonio, just a woman she had never set eyes on before telling her that they had gone away. She went back to her car, stunned and totally baffled. What the devil was going on? How could this have happened?

It took her less than two seconds to decide that there was an easy way to find out, for there could be only one person behind the pair's convenient disappearance. Livid with anger, she twisted the key in the ignition. It was time to pay Matthew Allenby a visit.

Caterina had never been to Matthew's villa before, but she knew where it was—high on the hills above Rino, with a magnificent view out over the bay. One of the grandest villas in the area, it was set in an acre of glorious garden, and as she drew up fifteen minutes later outside the front door the night air all around was filled with the sweet scent of the jasmine that covered the honey-coloured walls.

But Caterina noticed none of this as she sprang from the car and strode angrily across the crunchy gravel driveway—though she did notice that Matthew's silver Jaguar was parked outside. Well, at least it didn't look as though *he'd* conveniently disappeared!

She marched up to the front door and laid her finger on the bell. She waited, and was just about to ring again when the door was pulled open by a woman in a maid's uniform.

'I want to see Mr Allenby,' Caterina told her from between her teeth, not bothering to introduce herself.

The woman recognised her anyway. Looking startled, she invited, 'Please come inside. I'll see if he's available.'

Oh, he's available all right, Caterina fumed to herself silently as she stepped over the threshold and the woman closed the door behind her before hurrying off across the polished hallway. If he's not I'll come and dig him out with my bare hands!

Restlessly she paced the hallway, totally oblivious to her surroundings, which happened to include a fine Gobelin tapestry, an elegant boulle cabinet and a rare Canova sculpture, all of which in less fraught circumstances she would have felt moved to admire. And she was just starting to think that maybe she *would* have to go and dig him out when a sudden movement behind her made her spin round. And there he was, as large as life, standing at the foot of the wide marble staircase.

'Well, this is a surprise,' he said, smiling. 'Good evening.'

Caterina's heart had stopped inside her. All her fury had vanished. In an instant she was swept back to his office this afternoon. She was back in his arms and he was kissing her. Like a fool, she stopped scowling and simply smiled back at him instead.

'Good evening,' she responded, suddenly without a clue as to why she had come here, but rather glad that she had as he began to step towards her. And he really was looking even more delicious than usual, his hair a trifle rumpled, the buttons of his shirt undone. As she looked at him she was filled with a fierce and reckless longing to throw herself into his arms and kiss him.

'So, what can I do for you?' He had come to stand before her. 'Perhaps I can get you a drink for a start?'

What a splendid idea. Resisting her reckless urges, Caterina nodded demurely. 'OK. A martini, please. I like them—'

But that was as far as she got. For suddenly, over his shoulder, her eyes had alighted on a half-naked apparition standing at the top of the marble staircase. As, transfixed, she stared at it, the apparition spoke.

'*Chéri*,' it murmured, addressing Matthew, 'I'm feeling lonely. Come back to bed.'

## CHAPTER FIVE

YOU could have heard a pin drop.

Matthew, who hadn't been aware, until the moment she'd spoken, of the arrival on the scene of his half-naked girlfriend, turned round with commendable calm to look at her.

'Claire,' he said quietly, 'go and get dressed.'

Caterina, for her part, was incapable of speech. She just stared at the girl, who still stood at the top of the stairs dressed only in a lacy bra that perfectly flattered her generous curves and a pair of matching briefs for which the name could have been invented. And as she stared a thousand thoughts were flying through Caterina's head, though the uppermost of these was the absolute necessity not to reveal by her expression her sense of total numb shock. She felt as though a mine had just blown up in her face.

Claire hadn't so much as even glanced at Caterina. Her eyes were fixed on Matthew as she leaned against the banister in what could only be described as a Pirelli calendar pose.

'Come, *chéri*,' she purred in her sex-kitten voice. 'Come back up to bed. I'm lonely without you.'

Caterina was wondering if Matthew was having to control his expression too, for it was quite remarkable how calm and unfazed he was looking. Though perhaps there was just a hint of anger in his eyes.

He said again, his tone flat, 'Claire, go and get dressed.' And though he remained perfectly still there was something in his demeanour that warned very clearly that if she didn't do as she was told he would climb the stairs and remove her bodily.

Claire evidently understood this. She tutted with annoyance. Then, with a lazy, languid sigh, she detached herself from the banister and headed back to wherever it was she'd come from. Though not before pausing to throw Matthew a kiss over her shoulder.

'What a nasty, horrid bully you are,' she pouted.

As she disappeared, Matthew turned to face Caterina again. 'I apologise for the interruption.' He was as cool as a cucumber. 'I believe I was about to offer you a drink?' To look at him, you would have thought nothing out of the ordinary had happened.

Well, he could pretend that if he liked, but Caterina was not about to do likewise.

'My,' she said, in a tone that could have cut paper, 'I must say I wasn't expecting a floor show.'

'No, that was rather a surprise. Definitely not on the agenda.' Matthew smiled a composed smile. 'Let's go through to the drawing room, then I can fix you that drink and you can tell me why you've come.' And he turned on his heel and began to head across the hall.

Caterina did not follow him. She stood right where she was. 'Are you really sure you want to?' she demanded to his back. 'I got the impression you had unfinished business upstairs.' For now, of course, she knew why he was looking a little rumpled. He'd been interrupted while making love to Claire.

He cast her a cool look over his shoulder. 'Don't worry,' he assured her. 'I can finish it later. However,' he added, 'I appreciate your concern.' And, with that, he disappeared through the drawing-room doorway.

Caterina followed him. She was beginning to recover from her shock now, but her insides still felt as though they'd been fed through a mincer, and her emotions, quite frankly, were all over the place. And though she was vaguely aware of having had some purpose in coming here she could not for the life of her recall what it had been.

The only thing on her mind, the only thing she wanted an answer to, was the question of Claire and Claire's relationship with Matthew—the relationship he'd told Caterina was over and done with. What a perfectly abominable liar he was!

As she stepped into the drawing room he was standing by a small table on which an assortment of bottles and decanters was arranged. He glanced up at her as he poured a small whisky for himself.

'I believe you said you would like a martini?'

Caterina hesitated for a moment. It was true that she had said that, but she wasn't sure if she was in the mood for cosy drinks any more. Though maybe a drink wasn't a bad idea. It might help to pull her thoughts together. So she said, 'Yes, a martini. Extremely dry, please.'

Matthew reached for the cocktail shaker. 'Why don't you take a seat?'

That was another good idea, for her legs had turned to powder. So she seated herself in one of the armchairs behind her, leaning back against the cushions and crossing her legs casually, striving to look as relaxed and in control as he was.

No easy task. He seemed totally unruffled as he tossed ice into the shaker then splashed in gin and vermouth, gave it a couple of shakes and deftly poured the cocktail, along with a fat green olive, into a long-stemmed crystal glass. And as she watched him Caterina observed that he was almost as good at that as Leone. Her adored second brother was a real expert at mixing martinis.

Matthew was coming towards her now, holding out her glass to her. 'OK,' he said, sitting down on the armchair opposite her and taking a mouthful of his whisky. 'Let's hear to what I owe this unexpected pleasure.'

Caterina didn't even try to remember what that had been. Instead, she said what was on her mind, feeling a rush of anger as she did so, her tone tight and full of accusation.

'So much for your claim that your affair with Claire is over. I must say it doesn't look very over to me.'

Matthew laid down his glass and regarded her in silence, feeling a sharp pang inside him at the distress in her face. And for a moment he forgot the anger seething inside him, for he was really far from feeling as calm as he appeared.

Then he leaned forward. 'Look, Caterina, now's not the time for explanations. But I promise that what I said to you earlier today was true.' His tone was earnest, the expression in his eyes appealing. 'Appearances, as I've told you before, are not always what they seem.'

'Hah!' That was a good one! Caterina laughed a harsh laugh. Surely he didn't actually expect her to fall for that? She fixed him with a hard look and said in a tone to match, 'I wouldn't disagree that that can sometimes be the case. But I'm afraid there are some appearances that really can't be interpreted as being anything other than precisely what they seem!'

'I can assure you this isn't one of them.'

'You can assure me, can you? Well, I'm afraid I would say that when a half-naked girl appears from a man's bedroom and demands that he immediately return to bed there really aren't a whole lot of interpretations that would immediately spring to most people's minds.'

Breathless, she took a quick mouthful of her martini—which was perfectly delicious, quite as good as Leone's!

Matthew watched her, keeping a tight hold on his emotions. What had happened was a mess. A total disaster. But he could easily explain it all, there was no problem about that, and it was tempting just to go ahead and do so right now. But he must do it properly, calmly, without fear of interruption, and that was impossible now with Claire up to heaven knew what upstairs. No, he must stay cool and keep his explanations till later. He must wait till some other time to convince her.

But convince her he would. That was essential.

He took another mouthful of his whisky. 'What I think you should do right now is tell me the reason why you've come here.' His eyes glided over her tight, flushed face that he hated to see so full of hurt and confusion, especially since it was he who was the cause of it all. He said kindly, in an effort to lighten the atmosphere and maybe even coax the glimmer of a smile from her, 'I take it you weren't just passing and decided to drop in?'

Caterina, in her fraught state, totally misinterpreted his kindness. So now, she thought angrily, he's being condescending! She took a quick, angry slug of her perfect martini. Well, thank you very much but she didn't need that!

She straightened in her seat, feeling her anger swell inside her—and that was when it all suddenly came rushing back to her. Her appointment with Carla and Antonio. The empty house when she'd got there. Her furious drive across the city. The reason why she'd come here.

She glared at him. 'What have you done with Carla and Antonio?'

'Carla and Antonio?'

'Orazio's sister and her husband. Please don't try to tell me you don't know what I'm talking about.'

But Matthew was looking quite baffled. 'I'm afraid I don't,' he told her. 'What have these people got to do with me? Why would you think I'd done anything with them?'

Well, this was typical. This was what she'd half expected. Caterina laid down her glass before it shattered in her hand, for she was holding it so tightly now that it was in serious danger.

'You're trying to tell me you don't even know what I'm talking about?' And she gave him a look that would have cut a lesser man to ribbons.

But Matthew merely shrugged. 'Yes, I'm afraid I am.'

There was silence for a moment as Caterina continued to glare at him. What a liar, she was thinking. He just lied about everything. And he did it so well. He looked so damned convincing. Which was hardly surprising, of course, considering how much practice he got!

Then she took a deep breath. OK, she would play it his way. She sat back in her chair again and composed herself carefully. 'In that case, since you know nothing, let me explain the situation to you...'

She reached for her drink, took a mouthful and laid it down again. What a farce, she was thinking. As though he needs to have anything explained! Then, in a calm tone, watching him closely, she continued, 'This evening, as I suspect you already know, I had an appointment with Carla and Antonio. But when I got to their house—guess what? They weren't there.'

'You mean they'd gone out?'

'No, I mean they'd disappeared. There was this woman there I'd never seen before and she told me they'd gone, that they'd left San Rinaldo altogether.' She peered at him. 'Don't you think that's rather strange?'

'It is a bit. Are you sure she was telling the truth?'

What a game he was playing! She felt like walking across and hitting him. Instead, she counted very slowly to ten then replied, 'It looked as though she was. I searched the house from top to bottom. There was definitely no sign of them and all their things were gone.'

'You searched the house?' His eyebrows lifted.

'Yes, I did.' Caterina did not elaborate. It would amuse him no end to know how she'd pushed past the woman, who'd had no intention of allowing her over the threshold, and scoured the empty house in a state of near frenzy.

Matthew was watching her with a critical eye. 'My,' he observed, 'you must have been keen to keep this appointment. Your mission, whatever it was, was obviously very important.'

'Yes, it was. Very important.' And she fixed him with a dark look. For she was as mad as hell that, thanks to him, it had also been a total failure.

But then he surprised her. The iron-grey eyes narrowed. 'You must be exceedingly keen to see him again...'

Caterina said nothing for a moment. So he still believed that. She had wondered if that was the case when she had gone to the house and found it empty, but he would surely not have acted solely to stop her renewing her romance with Orazio? He was far too motivated by self-interest for that. The only reason why he would have intervened was to shield his own back.

So it would appear that he believed two things—that she was trying to contact Orazio, and that if she succeeded it would bode ill for him. Perhaps he hadn't believed that she had all the evidence in her possession, or had mistakenly judged that she wouldn't make a move without Orazio, and so had taken measures to stop her.

And stop her he had. Where on earth would she go from here? For she hadn't a clue where Carla and Antonio had gone. The woman at the house had refused to tell her a thing.

She felt a snap of anger inside her. 'Damn you for interfering! Why do you have to keep interfering in my life?' Then, when he said nothing, just looked at her, she stormed on angrily, 'There are laws in this country, you know, and you're not above them! You can't just make people disappear and get away with it!'

'I haven't made anyone disappear, though I can't say I'm sorry that these particular individuals have vanished. The further away they've gone the better, I'd say.'

'No doubt you would!' Caterina regarded him with distaste. Then she sat forward in her seat. 'What have you done with them?'

'Done with them? I've done nothing with them, as I've already told you.'

'I don't believe you! You've done something! They left because of you. Did you threaten them or something? What did you say to them? They wouldn't just suddenly disappear!'

Throughout this fusillade of accusations, Matthew hadn't batted an eyelid. He looked into her face. 'You've got it all wrong, you know.' Then he smiled. 'However, since you're clearly into that sort of thing, you're free to search the house, if you wish.'

Very funny. That simply made her madder. 'Don't kid yourself. I'll get to the bottom of this,' she warned him, not at all certain how she would ever manage such a thing. 'And I'll find them and I'll—'

She stopped herself. She had been about to say too much. And she was forgetting, too, about the agreement they'd made. She'd promised to do nothing against him as long as he withdrew from the job—except that she no longer had any intention of sticking to that. Still, it would be unwise to tell him. She clamped her mouth shut.

Matthew was leaning towards her, a frown furrowing his brow. He knew what she wanted to do to him, but he knew also that she would never do it. It simply was not within her power. But what he didn't know was how Orazio fitted into the picture. Was she really still in love with him? Was she planning to start their affair again? If this were so it would be a major obstacle to his plans.

He urged her, 'Go on, tell me. What will you do?'

'Nothing.'

'Nothing?' He looked into her closed face. 'I don't believe you, Caterina. What will you do?'

It was the strangest thing. She'd been glaring across at him, thinking how much she hated him, how she would teach him a lesson, and then suddenly, unexpectedly, he had spoken her name. And it had sounded so intimate—almost as though he had laid a hand on her—that all at once she had felt her skin tingle deliciously and a warm flush gather round the back of her neck.

As she looked at him, he said mildly, 'Is Orazio at the bottom of all this?'

Caterina did not answer. She had barely heard the question. All she was aware of was that her anger had suddenly fled from her, fallen in a soft, billowy heap at her feet. Her eyes strayed to his mouth and something twisted inside her as she remembered how it had felt against hers when he had kissed her. It was such a wonderfully sexy mouth. She longed to feel his kiss again.

But he had asked her something and now he was waiting for her answer. What was it? Oh, yes, he had asked about Orazio. And suddenly she wanted very much to tell him the truth. Orazio meant nothing to her. Her heart was as free as a bird.

But it was at that precise moment, just as she was about to tell him, that Claire came striding into the room.

Well, not exactly striding. Striding would have been out of the question in the narrow-cut slip of a dress she was wearing. It was more of a glide than a stride. Her legs barely seemed to move, but suddenly she was perched on the arm of Matthew's chair.

She leaned seductively towards him and breathed into his ear, curling one slender, milk-white arm around his neck. 'You bad boy,' she purred, 'leaving poor me all on my own like that upstairs.'

Caterina had gone quite stiff. It was as though a knife had been driven through her. Over the past few minutes she had entirely forgotten about Claire, and now, as she stared at the scene before her, she was having to struggle very hard to get her breath back. And little wonder, really. It was a pretty breathtaking scene.

The dress Claire was wearing... well, it was really only technically a dress. In truth it was no more than a wisp of blue silk chiffon that you could easily have rolled up and slipped into your pocket and still have had room left for your wallet and keys. This dress was so tiny and so full of slits and plunges that she really needn't have bothered to put it on at all. As she leaned against Matthew her breasts were almost falling out on top of him and there was enough thigh on display to have made a bishop kick in a stained-glass window.

What was on Matthew's mind was not at all apparent, though he did appear to be enduring this onslaught with remarkable stoicism. He neither pushed Claire away nor told her to behave—in fact did none of the things Caterina would have liked him to do. And she had missed the flash of anger that had touched his eyes a moment ago. She'd been so busy looking at Claire that she hadn't seen his jaw tighten.

As before, Claire hadn't glanced even once in her direction. It would appear, Caterina thought, that I've suddenly become invisible. And all at once she'd had enough. Let Matthew do as he pleased. Personally, all she wanted was to get out of here.

She rose stiffly to her feet. 'I think I'll leave now,' she announced, addressing no one in particular. Then, feeling as if she was made of wood, she turned towards the door.

Matthew did not try to stop her. He rose to his feet too. 'I'll see you out,' he told her. Then he paused and turned to Claire, who had got up with him, almost as though she were a part of him, or stuck to his side with miracle glue, and gently unravelled her arms from his neck.

'You stay here,' he said. 'I'll be back in a second.' And because his back was turned, Caterina was unaware of the look of angry warning that almost crackled in his face. 'Just stay here until I get back.'

Caterina watched the scene. Oh, don't worry, she was thinking. She'll wait for you all right. Probably upstairs in bed. And she was a little taken aback at the knife of sudden jealousy that went plunging through her at that thought. She didn't care. She didn't give a damn what the two of them got up to.

'Goodbye,' she said to Claire, knowing the girl wouldn't bother to answer. Then she turned sharply on her heel and headed out into the hallway. I'm suffocating, she was thinking. I need to get some air.

Matthew was right behind her. In fact, he reached the front door ahead of her and pulled it open, standing back as she stepped outside.

'I'm sorry about that,' he told her, though Caterina wasn't really listening. The last thing she was interested in was hearing his apologies. But she did hear him add, 'I think you and I need to talk. I'll come by your office tomorrow morning.'

She turned to shoot him a look of warning. 'Don't bother,' she told him. 'There's nothing you could have to say to me that I would even remotely want to hear.'

Then she swung away sharply before he could stop her, almost running across the gravel, heading for her car, gulping in great lungfuls of cool, cleansing air. Just let me out of here! every inch of her seemed to be crying.

She drove fast back to the palace, eyes fixed on the road ahead, desperately trying to think of nothing, struggling with all her strength to block out the images that were pouring in a tormented stream through her head.

But there was one image that, in spite of her struggles, she could not block out. One image that, the more she fought it, simply grew more vivid and clear. The image of Claire sprawled ripe and ready in Matthew's bed, the blue chiffon dress discarded on the floor.

OK. This was it. The chips were down. The gloves were off.

It was a couple of hours later and Caterina was lying in bed, a slow fuse burning inside her as she stared into the darkness. She had known she wouldn't sleep, but lying awake had proved useful. She had finally got a lot of things straight in her head.

Matthew Allenby was no good. He was a crook and a liar. By some devious means or other he had got rid of Carla and Antonio to stop her laying her hands on the evidence against him. And it seemed pointless to try to search for them. Where would she begin? She didn't know any of their friends and they had no relatives in San Rinaldo.

Besides, the chances were that they no longer had the evidence anyway. Matthew was hardly the type to go in for half measures. He'd probably stolen it from them and hidden it somewhere safe or destroyed it.

Her mind ranged over all the despicable things she knew about him. His devious, dishonest business dealings. His shameless social climbing. The wicked lies he'd invented about Orazio.

And that wasn't all, of course. He'd also lied about Claire.

Razors slashed at her insides as the image sprang up again, the image of the blue chiffon dress on the floor, its naked, nubile owner being ravished by Matthew on the bed. And it was shocking how much it hurt. She could barely breathe for a moment, every nerve-end ripped apart beneath the unbearable lash of jealousy.

She lay very still for a moment. She must conquer this madness. For somewhere along the line she had definitely been seized by madness. She had allowed herself to fall for him, to be bewitched by the powerful charm of him. And she must put an end to this dangerous folly. She must put an end to it at once.

For he would seduce her. She knew it. And she would allow him to. She would fight him for a bit and then she would give in. She would fall into his arms, and into his bed, like a ripe plum.

And that was why she had told Anna to wake her early tomorrow morning. She would go to see Damiano in his office first thing—without bothering to phone first, in case he tried to fob her off—and this time, even though she still had no evidence to show him, she would absolutely demand that he listen to what she had to say to him. And she would not leave till she had convinced him that Matthew Allenby must be dealt with.

At last, she could feel sleep begin to steal up on her. She closed her eyes and rolled over, hugging the big soft pillow beneath her head. Matthew Allenby was on borrowed time now. What a lovely thought to go to sleep with.

But then a strange thing happened. An image sprang into her head. An image of a girl sitting on Matthew's bed wearing nothing but a flimsy blue chiffon dress. And Matthew reaching out towards her with those sexy, sinuous hands of his and delicately, but hungrily, dropping the straps from her shoulders, exposing her full, high, thrusting breasts.

Now he was taking hold of those breasts and the girl was smiling and sighing and, as the image seemed to shimmer, Caterina, in her bed, smiled too. For the girl was not Claire. Inexplicably, she was Caterina. And the breasts that thrust so eagerly against Matthew's fingers were Caterina's.

She sighed again and hugged the pillow a little more tightly. Then, still smiling, she drifted off to sleep.

Caterina wasn't smiling when she awoke a few hours later. Instead, there was a determined frown on her face, last night's fleeting fantasy totally forgotten, the only thing in her head the meeting she was planning with Damiano.

She showered and dressed quickly, snatched a hurried cup of coffee, then, her jaw set and her fists clenched determinedly at her sides, set off for the west wing and the Duke's private quarters, praying that he would be there, that he hadn't gone off to some early appointment.

The door of his office was open. She swept through without knocking. Then, with a brief, 'Good morning,' she was sweeping past his secretary and heading for the door to his private inner sanctum. And her heart squeezed with triumph. He was here. She had caught him. He was seated at his desk beneath the priceless Canaletto, busily studying a pile of papers.

Caterina strode straight up to him. 'Damiano, I've got to speak to you. About something important. And I have to speak to you now.'

He paused and looked up at her with eyes as black as midnight. Eyes just like their father's, the late Duke, Caterina always thought, for they burned with the same intense raw passion. Though, sadly, it was a long time since they had last looked at her with the love and warmth that had been so typical of their father and that once, too, had shone in Damiano's eyes for her.

He said, 'I'm sorry, Caterina, but I'm really very busy.'

Caterina pushed away the hurt that had momentarily risen up inside her and concentrated hard on the reason why she had come here. In a firm tone she told him, 'I don't care how busy you are. I need half an hour of your time. It's very important.' And she planted herself in front of him as though nothing would budge her.

Damiano did smile then, though it was a smile with little humour. It was the half-tolerant smile he reserved for his wayward younger sister.

'Very well. If you insist. But I can't give you half an hour.' He glanced quickly at the slim gold watch at his wrist. 'Fifteen minutes is the most I can spare.'

'OK.'

Caterina breathed a sigh of relief and, with a small, triumphant smile, she seated herself quickly in one of the chairs that faced his desk. She had no idea that just seventeen minutes later, when she rose from that chair and walked out the door again, she would be wishing this meeting had never taken place.

Caterina was sitting alone on one of the stone benches that surrounded the fountain in the east-wing gardens of the palace, staring without seeing at the spray of splashing water that sparkled like crushed diamonds in the bright summer sunshine.

She'd had to get away after that meeting with her brother. To be alone. To think. To pull herself together. For he had told her things that had shocked her to her foundations. She was still having difficulty taking them in.

Though she knew they were true. Damiano had shown her proof of that. No wonder she was feeling sick to her soul.

As she sat there on her stone bench, a sad and vulnerable figure, she was totally unaware that, at the end of the gravel pathway, a man had suddenly appeared and was watching her curiously. Neither did she notice that he had started to walk towards her, his steps measured and purposeful, his expression intense, the iron-grey eyes never leaving her for an instant. And she was still totally oblivious when he came to a halt right beside her. It was only when he suddenly spoke that she realised he was there.

'Are you all right?' he asked her. 'Is something the matter?'

Startled, Caterina looked up. Matthew! Her heart faltered. She didn't feel like seeing anyone and certainly not him.

She stumbled to her feet. 'I'm fine. I was just going.' And she was about to turn round and flee in the opposite direction. Anywhere. Away from him.

But he stopped her. He reached out and caught her arm gently. He said, 'You don't look fine to me.'

Caterina turned to protest, to demand that he release her, but as she looked into his face and saw the sympathy and concern there her throat closed up with emotion and she found she could not speak. She turned her face away and stared at the ground.

Matthew took hold of both her arms now, drawing her towards him. 'Caterina,' he said, 'please tell me what's wrong.'

She wanted to pull away, but she hadn't the strength to. Biting her lip, she shook her head, terrified to look at him, fighting back the tears that threatened to spill.

But he was insisting. He shook her gently. 'Caterina,' he said again. Then again, 'Caterina, please tell me what's wrong.'

She did look at him then, and felt something crack inside her.

'Oh, Matthew!'

With a helpless sob, she fell into his arms.

# CHAPTER SIX

CATERINA wasn't at all sure how it had happened, but as she felt his arms go round her, drawing her close to him, all she was aware of was an enormous sense of release. Gratefully, she sank against him and let the scalding tears flow.

And Matthew didn't say a word. He just held her gently, stroking her back with strong, sure fingers as though he were comforting a frightened puppy.

The tears were soon over. Caterina drew away. She wiped her face with her hand. 'I'm sorry about that,' she said.

'No need to be sorry. You don't have to apologise.' The iron-grey eyes smiled at her. 'I'm just glad I happened to be around.'

It was odd, but Caterina was feeling rather glad now too. And she felt no shame or embarrassment at her emotional outburst, possibly because she was aware that he felt none either. Lots of people, especially men, got tight and awkward when faced with tears. But there wasn't a shred of anything like that in Matthew.

He took her arm now. 'Let's go for a walk. Then you can tell me what's troubling you, if you feel like it.' He smiled. 'And if you don't we'll just sit somewhere for a while until you're feeling a little more calm.'

Caterina made no protest, just let him guide her across the garden, past the narrow stone-flagged path that led to the private chapel, then down to the lake, half-hidden behind the trees, where a pair of swans glided on water as smooth as glass.

He seemed to have guaged her mood precisely and to know just what she needed, for as she walked Caterina began to feel calmer. And she was grateful that he wasn't plying her with questions. She wasn't sure if she wanted to share what had upset her.

'Shall we sit here for a while?' They were down at the lake's edge. 'We could sit under that tree. It might be more comfortable in the shade.'

'OK.' Caterina nodded and followed as he led the way. Then she seated herself, with a soft sigh, beneath the shady branches, curled her legs beneath her and gazed down at the lake.

Matthew gazed down at the lake too, and for a moment neither of them spoke. The only sounds were the occasional plop as a duck dived for weed at the lake bottom and the soft, gentle rustling of leaves above their heads.

Then, as the pair of swans came into view, Matthew suddenly said, 'You know, when I was a little boy there was a lake near where I lived where a pair of swans used to come every year to mate. Every spring it was a major excitement waiting for them to arrive.'

As he paused, Caterina turned round to look at him, her blue eyes narrowing curiously as they fixed on his profile. For he was still gazing at the lake. He had not turned to look at her. And she found herself reflecting on something Damiano had told her in the course of their fateful seventeen-minute meeting—a cryptic remark he'd refused to enlarge on. 'There are a lot of things about Matthew Allenby that would surprise you if you knew them.' She sat back a little now and waited to hear what he would say next.

'They'd been coming for years.' He leaned back on one elbow and continued his story, still gazing at the lake. 'They mate for life, you know, swans. It's really quite remarkable. And if one of the pair dies the other will never mate again. The bond between them is unbreakable. They're totally devoted.'

'That sounds rather like my parents.' Caterina said it without thinking. And as Matthew turned to glance at her she sighed, realising she would have to explain, for it had all happened before he had arrived in San Rinaldo.

'My father died four years ago. My mother was devastated. They were very close, you see. They had a wonderfully happy marriage. And though there was absolutely nothing wrong with her she died in her sleep just a year later. I think she just didn't want to go on living without him.'

It felt strange and yet not strange to be telling him this about her parents. Her great loss was a subject she very rarely spoke about, for, to tell the truth, she still found it painful. But when he had spoken about the swans she had thought instantly of her parents, and somehow it had just felt right to share her thoughts with Matthew.

He said, 'Of course it's a tragedy when one of the two dies, but really we can only envy such couples.'

Caterina smiled back at him. 'That's what I've always thought,' she told him. And, as their eyes met, she was aware of a sudden warmth between them, an intuitive understanding far deeper than words. It was as though something had snuggled up, soft and reassuring, next to her heart.

Then she tilted her head at him. 'Go on with your story.'

Matthew smiled and turned back to gaze at the lake again. 'Well, one year,' he continued, 'only the cob—that's the male—arrived, and it was clear right away that there was something very wrong. He kept flapping about as though he was trying to tell us something. Flying off, then coming back. Over and over. Until one of the villagers decided we ought to follow him.'

He paused and pulled a blade of grass and chewed on it. 'What happened next was quite amazing. The cob led us to another lake about seven miles north of ours where he and his mate must have stopped off on their way. And there was his mate, very sick, apparently dying, lying half-hidden amongst the reeds.'

'Oh, no!' Caterina leaned forward, her brow puckering with concern. 'What had happened?' She was totally caught up in his story.

Matthew sighed. 'What had happened was that some irresponsible fisherman had left lying around one of those lead weights some of them use, and, as can tragically happen, the swan had swallowed it. And now she was slowly being poisoned to death.'

'How terrible! And did she die?' Caterina looked at him anxiously. She desperately wanted this story to have a happy ending.

Matthew turned to her and smiled. 'No, I'm glad to say, she didn't. The local vet was able to save her. He removed the lead weight and she made a full recovery. And that year, just as usual, we had our little brood of cygnets on the lake.'

'Oh, how wonderful!' Caterina sat back with a huge sigh of relief. 'And after that? Did the parents keep coming back every year as usual?'

'Just like clockwork, every year.'

Caterina shook her head and laughed. 'What a lovely story!' So unlike her own, she couldn't help thinking. She said, staring at the lake, 'When it comes to loyalty and common decency I reckon swans must be higher up the evolutionary scale than some men.'

Though she sensed that Matthew had turned to look at her she remained staring at the lake, not meeting his gaze as she continued, 'Earlier this morning I had a meeting with Damiano. To be honest, I went there to tell him a few things about you. But what happened was that *he* ended up telling *me* a few things instead, among them some rather nasty revelations about Orazio.' She sighed. 'I'm afraid it wasn't nearly as pretty as your swan story.'

If she had been looking at him, she would have seen the flash of understanding in Matthew's eyes. So that was what had happened. Damiano had told her about Orazio. He said nothing, just waited for her to go on.

Caterina leaned back in the grass, propping herself on one elbow. Suddenly, she wanted to tell him the whole story. In a way, perhaps, she even owed it to him to tell him.

'He told me something about Orazio that came as a total shock.'

She paused and bit her lip as emotion welled up inside her. Anger and shock and disappointment, plus a sense of deep hurt at the way it had all come out. For what Damiano had just told her he had told her without compassion, angrily, impatiently, brutally silencing her as soon as she had begun to pour out her complaints against Matthew. It was as though he simply hadn't cared that what he revealed might be painful. He had just dumped it all on her with no effort to be kind. And it was this, her brother's lack of kindness, that had devastated her soul.

She forced herself to speak. 'He told me,' she began, 'that Orazio used his relationship with me to try and blacken your name and get you thrown off the arts and crafts job. Apparently...' She took a deep breath. This part really made her sick. What a fool she had been ever to have trusted such a man. 'Apparently,' she continued, 'he was even being paid to do it.' She paused, swallowing her anger, and looked deep into Matthew's eyes. 'You knew all this already, didn't you?'

Matthew nodded. 'Yes, I did.' He'd known the whole story from the start.

'When they found out about our relationship,' Caterina continued, 'the firm you beat to get the job approached Orazio and offered him money to feed me lies against you. Lies I was then supposed to pass on to Damiano, so that he would fire you and give the job to them instead.' Her lips pursed in distaste. 'And Orazio took the money.' She laughed an awkward laugh. 'I guess you could say he used me.'

'In a way.'

'In a big way.' There was bitterness in her tone. 'He used me as his dupe.' She pulled a face. 'And what a dupe.'

Matthew regarded her kindly. 'Don't be hard on yourself,' he told her. 'Orazio is something of an expert at duping people.'

'Yes, so I've found out.'

She gazed down at the grass. Damiano had finally forced her to listen to what she had refused to listen to six months ago. And he had shown her evidence not only of what Orazio had been up to with her but of a whole string of other shady dealings as well.

And he'd told her, 'I would never have banned your relationship if I hadn't had proof of what kind of man he was. You ought to have known me better than that.'

He was right, of course. She ought to. One thing to be said for her brother was that he had never been a man to act on hearsay. But she'd been blind. She'd been stupid. She'd trusted Orazio and believed all his vicious stories about Matthew. It had never even occurred to her that Orazio might be the real villain.

She sighed now and looked at Matthew. 'I was wrong about you. You're not at all what Orazio told me you were.'

'I can assure you,' Damiano had told her, 'I had him thoroughly vetted, just like I vet everyone before I employ them, and he came out, I promise you, as clean as a whistle. You can take my word for it that all this so-called evidence Orazio told you he left with his sister was either faked or never existed. And, if you ask me, that's why Carla and Antonio disappeared. They probably contacted Orazio and told him what you were after and he simply advised them to make themselves scarce. He knows the game's up and he doesn't want any more trouble.'

So, it was all clear now. Now she understood why Orazio had made such a hasty exit—not to save her embarrassment, as he'd so generously claimed at the time, but simply because he'd known he'd been found out.

And now she also knew the truth about Matthew.

She'd felt shattered when Damiano had told her, though oddly unsurprised. But most of all what she'd felt was a fearful sense of relief. Relief to know that she had no more cause to hate him. Fear because not hating him left her defenceless and at his mercy.

She tried not to think of that now as she told him, 'I can only apologise for all the awful things I've said. I was totally in the wrong.' Though she had been right about one thing, and she fixed him now with a mock-accusing look. 'Damiano told me it was you who put him on to Orazio. You tipped him off as to what kind of man he was...'

Matthew did not deny it. 'I felt I had no choice, though I had no idea at the time that he had it in for me. But I knew he was a crook. One of my companies once had dealings with him, and I'm afraid I didn't consider him a suitable companion for the Duke's sister.' He frowned. 'All the same,' he told her, 'I very much regretted how the whole thing affected you.'

Caterina could see that he really meant that and she felt touched to the heart. He was so kind. That was something she hadn't realised before.

She told him, 'I can't really blame you. I reckon it was your duty to speak out.' Then she pulled a contrite face. 'You were also right, I realise now, about those garden-party invitations of mine that you disapproved of. Damiano told me those people were as bad as Orazio. It seems I was wrong from top to bottom.'

'It happens. We all make bad judgements,' he told her. 'Still, I'm glad my name's finally been cleared in your eyes. I always knew the truth would come out sooner or later, though I also knew there was no point in me trying to tell you.' The dark eyes searched deep into hers for a moment. 'Maybe now you and I can finally stop fighting? Who knows? Maybe we can even be friends?'

'Maybe.'

Caterina felt a thrust of emotion deep inside her. Friends? A simple notion with endless possibilities. Possibilities that both excited and profoundly scared her. And there was really nothing to stop her now from taking the fatal plunge, for not only did she know he was not the swindler she had thought he was, she now also had serious doubts about the rest.

For it seemed perfectly possible that Orazio had also been lying when he'd accused Matthew of being a shameless social climber. That could easily just have been part of the slander he'd been paid to invent. Matthew had never denied it, but that didn't mean anything. He'd never denied any of the other stuff either. And the more she thought about it, the more sure she felt that it had been a lie.

So she really was defenceless now. Except for one thing. Claire still stood between them. For he had definitely lied about Claire.

He was saying, 'So, does all this mean we can work together, after all?' He smiled. 'Or do you still want me to find that replacement while I'm in London?'

Again that thrust inside her. That excitement touched by fear. 'No,' she told him. 'I don't think that'll be necessary. There's no reason at all why we can't work together now.'

'Good. I look forward to it.'

Matthew hid a secret smile. He had never had any intention of finding a substitute. That had just been a ploy to put off forcing her hand, which, in the end, he suspected, had accidentally been forced by that unfortunate little scene with Claire last night. It was an outcome he had not anticipated, but it seemed like a very good sign.

That scene had obviously got to her, so perhaps, in spite of her attachment to Orazio, she was starting to feel something for him after all. He felt a lift inside him. He must build on this progress. He must steal her heart and make her his.

As he watched her she glanced quickly at her watch. Then she looked up at him. 'I think I'd better get moving now. I have an appointment in town in half an hour's time.' She began to rise to her feet. 'Thank you for listening. This little interlude by the lake was just what I needed.'

Matthew rose to his feet too. 'I'm glad I was here to listen.' Then he told her, 'If you're going back to the car park I'll come with you. I have to get into town for an appointment too.'

So, together, at a leisurely pace, they set off across the grass, then down the gravel pathway past the fountain, heading for the little courtyard where their cars were parked. And as they walked Caterina could sense a new easiness between them. They seemed to be perfectly in step, as though they understood each other at last. Happy warmth flooded through her. She liked this new feeling rather a lot.

They were approaching the courtyard when Matthew turned to her. 'I guess I won't be seeing you again until the birthday party on Friday. As you know, I'm off to London tomorrow.'

'Of course.' Though in fact Caterina had totally forgotten. And now she felt a shaft of disappointment. He would be gone for several days and she knew she would miss him.

She also felt something else—a sudden, searing lick of jealousy as Claire jumped into her mind and she wondered if she was going with him.

But she refused to think of Claire. Thinking of Claire would only spoil things. So she simply pushed her from her mind as they stepped into the courtyard where his low silver Jaguar was parked opposite her little red Honda.

She turned to him and smiled, extending her hand in farewell. 'So long for now, then. Have a good trip,' she told him.

'Thanks.'

He smiled back at her. But he did not take her hand. And suddenly there was a dark, smoky look in his eyes that had a perfectly cataclysmic effect on her. All at once she was remembering in shockingly vivid detail the fantasy she'd had last night before she'd drifted off to sleep.

Her sitting on Matthew's bed wearing nothing but a skimpy dress. Him reaching out and slipping the straps from her shoulders. Him, with gentle hunger, taking hold of her breasts. And all at once a flame of desire curled round her loins and she could feel her heart thundering like an express train in her chest.

'Goodbye,' she tried to say, but all that came out was a strangled croak.

'Goodbye, Caterina.'

At last, he took her hand. But he did not shake it. Instead, he simply held it. And then, very gently, he drew her towards him. A moment later his arms were round her and he was bending to kiss her lips.

Really, it was almost as brief and as fleeting as that first kiss, but there was a fire in his lips this time, an unmistakable hunger. And its effect on Caterina was powerful and instantaneous. It was as though something had exploded violently inside her. She felt a heat and a piercing sense of excitement pour through her. Breathlessly, she clung to him, feeling as if she was bursting into flames.

But it was over before it had begun. Cruelly, he was relaxing his grip on her, and she, remembering where they were, was doing the same.

He looked down at her. 'Till Friday,' he said. 'At the party.' And his eyes were dark and smoky with desire.

Caterina could scarcely bear to look at him. Every inch of her was in tumult. And she knew that if she looked too long into those eyes she would faint.

But he was already turning away. Even as she stood there, blinking and struggling to pull herself together, he was striding off towards the Jaguar.

Caterina staggered to her own car and stumbled inside. Then she sat very still and breathed slowly to compose herself. But it was a good few minutes, long after the Jaguar had driven off, before she'd stopped trembling enough to fit the key in the ignition.

It was a week later, the evening of Damiano's birthday party, and Caterina was in her rooms at the palace getting dressed.

At least, she was supposed to be getting dressed. She'd already had her bath, and Robert, her private hairdresser, had been up to fix her hair in the flattering half-up-half-down style he did so well. And in less than twenty minutes she was due to go downstairs and join the others in a celebratory glass of champagne before the dinner proper got under way. But the trouble was she couldn't decide what to wear.

'Let me try the green one again.' Then she laughed. 'Oh, Anna, I'm sorry! I know I've already tried it on at least a dozen times. I don't know what's wrong with me. I just can't make up my mind.'

Anna, who had been Caterina's personal maid for three years now and was immensely fond of her high-spirited young mistress, simply smiled a tolerant smile in response. 'That's no problem,' she assured her. 'But if you want my opinion the pink one is definitely the one you look best in.'

Caterina had thought that too, for there was no doubt about it—the deep *bois de rose* colour was immensely flattering. But perhaps the dress itself was just a little bit tame. Unlike the green one, which she'd bought on impulse only yesterday and which had the most boldly plunging neckline she'd ever worn in her life and was so close-fitting that it looked almost as though it had been sprayed on.

It wasn't her usual sort of thing, though she certainly had the figure for it, but it looked like the sort of thing that Matthew would go for. She was well aware of his penchant for provocatively dressed women!

'What do you think?' Having slipped it on for the ninth time at least, she twisted and turned in front of the mirror. 'The truth now, Anna. Do you think it's me or not?'

That was a hard one to answer, Anna reflected. There'd been such a change in her mistress over the past week, a definite softening after the slight brittleness of the last few months when it had seemed as though the only thing she cared about was work. A softening, and yet a coming back to life again as well. Her old sparkle was back and even more sparkling than before!

And she found herself pondering, I wonder who the man is? For when a woman suddenly blossomed like this there had to be a man in the picture somewhere!

She said, 'I'm not really sure. I think it's very striking.' Though she might have added that Caterina didn't need such a striking dress. A couple of months ago, perhaps. But certainly not this evening. This evening she was glowing with her own radiant inner glow.

Caterina, of course, was quite unaware of this. She regarded her reflection with a critical eye. Yes, she was thinking, Matthew would definitely approve of this—though at the same time she was trying hard to convince herself that the only reason why she wanted to wear it was because she liked it herself. There was definitely a bit of self-deception going on.

'I don't know...'

Still undecided, she turned to scan the other dresses that hung from the dressing-room doors and which she'd been trying on for over an hour—the red, the yellow, the black, the blue, and finally, lingeringly, the lovely *bois de rose*, which was really rather gorgeous, but so boring and demure.

She turned back to the mirror for a final confirmation. Yes, striking was the word. She'd knock him dead in this.

She turned back to Anna. 'Definitely this one. Now fetch me the green sandals—quick!—before I change my mind again!'

\* \* \*

In his bedroom at the villa, Matthew was getting ready for the party too, though he was suffering no such agonies about what to wear.

He was already dressed, except for the jacket of his black dinner suit, and he was adjusting the cuffs of his white dress shirt as he got ready to slip his cuff-links into place.

But it was as he picked the first one up that he was assailed by a sudden doubt. Normally, for a special occasion, these were the cuff-links he would wear, but perhaps tonight they might be out of place.

He glanced down at the glistening gold cuff-link in his hand with its armorial crest picked out in blue enamel. And he frowned. No, not tonight. Not with Caterina present. And he dropped it back into the little china dish on his dressing table and reached for the plain gold cuff-links instead. These, he decided, would be much more appropriate.

He glanced at his watch. It was time he was on his way. He crossed to the wardrobe, lifted his jacket from its hanger, slipped it on quickly and headed for the door. It was a fifteen-minute drive to the Palazzo Verde. No problem. He would make it in plenty of time.

It was a warm, balmy night and Matthew slid down the windows of the Jaguar as he headed down the drive and out to the main highway. He'd have time to take the Corniche, the road that skirted the glittering bay around which the capital city, Rino, was built. It was a little longer than the ring road but it was breathtakingly beautiful and he liked to take it whenever he could.

Besides, to be honest, he felt like spinning things out a bit, deliberately putting off the magic moment when he would reach the palace and see Caterina again.

And he smiled to himself, feeling that familiar clench inside him that he always felt these days whenever he thought of her. Excitement. Anticipation. A sense of urgency and impatience. A growing desire to make her his at last. It was funny, but just a very short while ago she hadn't figured in his plans for the future at all. But that had all changed now. Now she was at their very centre. And his future had taken on a whole new rosy glow.

As the low silver car, gleaming in the soft moonlight, swept down the palm-lined, curving Corniche, where couples strolled hand in hand or sat together on the wooden benches sharing dreams as they gazed out towards the horizon, he reflected on his strategy for the coming evening.

He must play it by ear, of course, for it would depend on her state of mind and whether she was still upset over what Damiano had told her about Orazio, but what he was banking on was that, somehow, he would have the opportunity to speak to her alone and finally convince her on the subject of Claire. That was essential if any further progress was to be made.

He thought about the day when he had gone to the palace early, partly to see Damiano, but principally to catch Caterina, precisely with the purpose of explaining about Claire.

He had been crossing the west-wing corridor when, through one of the windows, he'd seen her fleeing, clearly distressed, across the garden. He'd gone after her wondering what could possibly be the matter and had been shocked to discover just how stricken she was at Damiano's revelations about her ex-lover. So he had said nothing about Claire. That would have been out of place.

But now, mentally, he crossed his fingers. Perhaps things had changed. Over the past few days perhaps she'd finally come to terms with just how unworthy of her affections Orazio really was. And it was his task now somehow to find a way to drive that no-good from her heart for ever—and to convince her, once and for all, that Claire didn't figure in his.

At last he left the Corniche and began to drive inland again, up the broad, curving road that led to the Palazzo Verde, whose high, turreted walls beneath the glimmering starlight seemed suffused with an ancient rosy glow. And Matthew could feel his heart begin to beat a little faster. He had a feeling that tonight was going to be important.

The guards at the palace gates waved him through with a friendly salute, then he was heading for the palm-filled courtyard at the side of the palace to park his car in its usual place. There were a number of cars already parked beneath the palm trees. Clearly, some of his fellow guests had already arrived.

He made his way across the courtyard and through the big wooden doors to the entrance hall where a group of palace staff were waiting to greet the guests.

'Don't worry, I can find my own way,' he assured them with a smile. Then, as they nodded, he strode swiftly across the polished marble floor, heading for the staircase that led to the Blue Ballroom where Damiano's birthday party was taking place.

And, indeed, the reception was well under way as he stepped through the double doors, flanked by liveried footmen, into a gold-ceilinged room, lit with fabulous chandeliers, that was positively alive with bright colours and happy chatter. There were women in gorgeous ballgowns wearing glittering tiaras, men looking sleek in their immaculate DJs, while an army of waiters bearing heavy silver trays wove soundlessly amongst them, discreet and efficient, dispensing canapés and crystal flutes of the best champagne.

Matthew's first task, of course, was to greet Damiano. But, as he headed for the Duke, from the corner of his eye he was searching the sea of faces for Caterina. He could see Leone, her other brother, with his beautiful American wife Carrie, and he could see the Duchess, Sofia, looking as stunning as ever, but, alas, there appeared to be no sign of Caterina.

A filcker of dismay went through him. Maybe she wasn't coming. Maybe she was still too upset, still weeping for Orazio. And maybe all his plans and dreams would come to nothing. It was quite shocking just how shattered that prospect made him feel.

But as he reached Damiano's group and held out his hand to greet his host his attention was suddenly caught by a movement by the doors. He saw the footmen step aside. Someone was coming into the room.

'Matthew, welcome.'

'Good evening.' He nodded a salute. 'And may I wish you a very happy birthday.'

But, though he appeared to be functioning perfectly normally and Damiano never for one second suspected that his attention was elsewhere, the fact of the matter was that Matthew's heart had stood still at the sight of the vision in the *bois de rose* dress who, with a serene, glowing smile, was walking towards him.

## CHAPTER SEVEN

'So, how was London?'

'London was London.' He smiled. 'It rained.'

Caterina laughed. 'But even in the rain it's a beautiful city.'

Though right now, she was thinking, there could be no more beautiful sight than this magnificent man who was standing before her. For when she'd stepped through the doorway and spotted him with Damiano the already bright room had instantly grown brighter and her heart had flipped over like a pancake in her chest. I couldn't have borne another day without him, she'd thought.

Of course, she'd kept her feelings hidden as she'd crossed the room to greet her brother, but inside she'd been glowing like a thousand torches. It hadn't mattered that she'd known she was being an absolute idiot.

And thank heavens she'd changed her dress. To insist on the green one would have been catastrophic madness, not to say a trifle obvious. Though she'd been halfway down the corridor before she'd finally admitted to herself that she was committing a total and utter folly. The dress wasn't her. She felt uncomfortable and silly in it. She wasn't Claire and, what was more, she didn't want to be Claire. She'd simply have to take her chances on being who she really was.

So, she'd dashed back to her dressing room and informed a startled Anna, 'The pink one after all!

You were absolutely right. And I'll wear the gold and silver sandals.'

So what if the *bois de rose* dress was far from flashy—even, it might be said, a little on the demure side, with its wide round neck, little cap sleeves and tiny cinched-in waist accentuated by a single pink silk rose? If it failed to turn Matthew on, that was just too bad. No big deal. She could easily live with that.

Or could she? she was wondering now as they exchanged a few private words before moving through with the other guests to the huge elegant dining room. It made her ache just to look at him. It almost broke her heart. And it would be nice if he was aching just a little bit too.

He was telling her, 'It was a frantically busy week. I hardly stopped for breath all the time I was there, and I only got back a couple of hours ago.'

'But you achieved what you went for?'

Caterina was watching him closely, shamelessly feasting on those beautiful eyes, that glorious dark hair and that wonderful sexy mouth. Then a sudden thought struck her. *Had* Claire been with him? And she almost gasped at the sick, fierce clench in her stomach. But she pushed the thought away. She refused to think of Claire. Hadn't she decided that thinking of Claire only spoiled things?

'I had a very productive time. But I'm glad to be back.' He looked into her eyes and touched her arm lightly, and there was just a hint of urgency in his voice as he added, 'I hope we can manage to have a few private moments alone together later?'

'I should think so.' As her heart leapt, she bowed her head demurely. A few private moments alone together. It sounded like heaven.

He smiled at her. 'Good. I look forward to that.'

They had been placed at opposite sides of the huge mahogany table, which was laid with polished silver and baccarat crystal and a perfectly exquisite dinner service of local Castello porcelain which was an exact replica of the one that had been made for the first Duke back in 1670 and was kept locked up in the current Duke's private quarters. The whole table sparkled like an Aladdin's cave of treasures.

Caterina was seated just a few seats along from the Duke and Duchess, with the Lord Chamberlain on her left and the German ambassador on her right, both men she knew well and whose conversation she enjoyed. Though, of course, she would much rather have been sitting next to Matthew.

He was seated between a rather ravishing Romanian princess and the almost equally stunning wife of the Lord High Admiral, definitely two of the most beautiful women in the room. Perhaps that ought to be troubling her, she found herself reflecting, for it was clear, especially from the way the princess was flirting with him, that it would be easy for Matthew to forget all about her and concentrate his attentions on these two beautiful women instead.

But that wasn't going to happen. Somehow Caterina just knew that. For he kept glancing across at her, catching her eye and smiling. In spite of the competition, he seemed to have eyes only for her.

She thrilled inside. Something special was happening.

The meal passed in a blissful subdued excitement of these exchanged glances and smiles across the table. And Caterina, who never normally drank very much anyway, was careful to moderate her intake of wine.

She wanted to be perfectly sober, all senses clearly functioning, when they finally met in private after the dinner. Something flared inside her at the thought of being alone with him. He had said he was looking forward to it. She was looking forward to it too.

There was only one slightly sobering aspect to the evening, though probably only Caterina was aware of it, and that was the sad look she noted from time to time flitting across the young Duchess's face.

So nothing had changed, Caterina reflected. Damiano and Sofia's marriage was clearly as rocky as ever and poor Sofia was continuing to suffer. Caterina sighed, her heart going out to her young sister-in-law, and flicked a glance along at Damiano.

Of course, Damiano gave nothing away whatsoever. Her handsome black-eyed brother was just as poised and in control as he always was. But, as Caterina looked at him, she found herself wondering if the rumours she'd heard recently could possibly be true.

It was no secret that Damiano's marriage had been a marriage of convenience. When he'd inherited their father's crown just over four years ago he'd been a bachelor and, naturally, without heirs. That had had to be put right, so he'd married Sofia, the beautiful younger daughter of a local baron, and nine months ago she had presented him with the required son and heir. But the marriage itself seemed to have brought neither of them much happiness. And now the rumour was that Damiano had taken up again with Lady Fiona, his former long-time mistress.

Was it true? Caterina felt angry as she continued to watch him. She had always loved him dearly, but he could be so uncaring, so insensitive, as she knew all too well from personal experience these days. Didn't it matter to him that he was slowly breaking his young wife's heart?

But this was a party and there was Matthew, looking so utterly gorgeous across the table, so she didn't allow herself to dwell for too long on these sad thoughts. Instead, with growing impatience, she started to count the minutes to when the two of them would finally have some time alone together.

At last they reached the last course. The huge iced birthday cake, decorated with the Duke's crest and thirty-seven flickering candles, was brought in to a collective gasp of appreciation from the guests. There was a round of applause as Damiano blew out all the candles. Then coffee was served, and as the tall French doors that led on to the huge terrace were pushed open some of the guests rose from the table and drifted outside to take their coffee out of doors.

Matthew caught Caterina's eye and signalled that they should do likewise. Pausing only to excuse herself politely from her two neighbours, Caterina rose to her feet, suddenly dying with excitement. Then, controlling her impatience, struggling desperately to look casual, she made her way out onto the moonlit terrace where a delicious fresh breeze was drifting up from the sea, adding a sweet-salty tang to the balmy night air.

Positioning herself by the balustrade where he would easily see her, she waited for him to appear through the open doorway and claim her.

But where was he? Minutes ticked by and still there was no sign of him. What had happened? Had she misunderstood his signal?

She peered anxiously around her at the groups gathered on the terrace. Had he missed her? Was she waiting for him in the wrong place, perhaps? Her eyes darted back to the open doorway. Maybe he was still inside? Should she go back in and check?

But then she froze to the spot, for suddenly she'd spotted him.

It was just a glimpse, but just a glimpse was more than enough. He was walking across the dining room. And suddenly she felt quite sick. At his side was the ravishing Romanian princess.

The world that had seemed so bright was suddenly plunged into darkness. Blind with misery, her legs turned to cardboard beneath her, Caterina turned away and leaned against the balustrade. So she had been wrong after all to discount *everything* as lies. That had clearly just been wishful thinking on her part. The bit about his social climbing tendencies was sadly true and he just hadn't been able to resist the lure of a princess. After all, that was definitely a couple of steps from a mere lady!

That made her feel even worse, for if it was true where did it leave her? Had he really only been interested in her for what he could gain from the relationship? Her heart seemed to wither with pain inside her. She'd been trying so very hard not to even consider that possibility.

She stared unseeingly across the gardens, struggling to pull herself together. At last the blackness passed and she began to feel more in control again. She straightened, firming her shoulders. She'd put him out of her mind now and go and join one of the groups chatting on the terrace. Chin up, quite composed, she started to swing round.

And almost walked straight into Matthew.

'I'm sorry I kept you waiting.' He had taken her lightly by the arm. 'In spite of my protests, my dinner companion insisted on introducing me to her father. Apparently, he lived for many years in London and can't let an Englishman go by without having a word.' He smiled a contrite smile. 'I got away as quickly as I could.'

Was all that true? The question flickered in Caterina's mind for only a split second. Then she smiled and gave way to the relief rushing through her, casting aside her fears and embracing with joy the sheer delirious magic of looking into his face again.

'That's OK,' she said lightly. 'I was just admiring the view.'

Some lie, she thought wryly, recalling her moment of anguish, that blackness that had descended on her, that sense of hopelessness and despair. It had passed quickly enough, but while it had lasted it had crushed her. And thinking back on it now she found it all rather scary. She'd had no idea she was capable of such out-of-control feelings.

'How about taking a walk down to the lake to see those swans of ours?'

Caterina slipped her arm through his as though it was the most natural thing in the world. And it was funny, Caterina reflected, but that was precisely how it felt.

'Why not?' she agreed. And she tried to douse the silly pleasure that she'd felt when he'd said 'those swans of ours'. It felt terribly special that they should have something they shared.

'So, how did you enjoy the dinner party?'

They were heading down the path beneath the trees, whose branches seemed touched with silver in the moonlight. Caterina felt as though she was being transported to heaven.

'I thought it was great and everyone seemed to enjoy themselves.' She'd been vaguely aware of that through her own giddy euphoria. She laughed. 'Fancy Damiano being thirty-seven!'

'That's not so old. I'll be thirty-seven, too, in a couple of years.' Matthew squeezed her hand. 'Just because you're the baby of the family.'

'I guess I am.' She laughed. 'My parents always claimed I was an afterthought.'

'A pretty special afterthought.'

As the grey eyes turned to look at her, Caterina felt a blush fly to her cheeks. That look in his eyes, dark and smoky and full of promises, seemed to caress her like a finger.

She took a gulp of air and asked him, genuinely curious, 'Were you an afterthought too? I bet you weren't.'

'I don't know what I was. I guess I just sort of happened.' He flicked another look at her and smiled a humorous smile. 'I happened right in the middle. I have two older sisters and two younger brothers.'

'Really?'

She'd never thought of him having brothers and sisters and she found this new concept inordinately fascinating. She longed to ask him all about them. Who they were. What they did. She longed to reach into his life and find out all about him. And she remembered once again what Damiano had told her—that there were a lot of things about Matthew that would surprise her if she knew them. She was filled with an immense urge to discover what they were.

But they had reached the edge of the lake now and before she could ask him anything he was pointing across the water, which shone like a mirror.

'Look,' he told her. 'There are our swans.'

That 'our' had the same delicious effect as before. A shiver of warm pleasure went rippling through her. 'So they are,' she smiled, her eyes following where he was pointing, though her mind wasn't really on the swans at all. All she could think of was the tall masculine presence at her side.

'Aren't they beautiful?' As Matthew spoke, he slipped an arm around her waist.

It was really only at that moment, as she felt the warmth of him against her, that Caterina fully realised just how desperate her longing was. She melted against him and remained very still. Hardly daring to breathe. Not daring at all to look at him. Her heart was pounding like a hammer against her ribs.

'Not as beautiful as you, however.'

He had turned ever so slightly. And though she still did not glance up she could feel him looking down at her. The iron-grey eyes seemed to burn into her face.

'Earlier, when you first arrived and I suddenly saw you walking across the room, I thought you were the most beautiful thing I'd ever seen.'

He had turned more fully to face her. With his free hand he touched her hair.

'That dress you're wearing... it suits you like a dream.'

As he paused, Caterina dared to glance up at last. And as she looked into his eyes, as dark and endless as the sky, she was filled with such a sense of exquisite anguish that she half feared she might literally melt into the ground. Her poor bewildered heart felt like a ball of fire within her. She had never felt anything like this before in her life.

Matthew continued to gaze down at her while, very softly, with the backs of his fingers, he caressed the side of her face.

'Caterina,' he said, making her stomach shrink to nothing.

And then, at last, he was taking hold of her and drawing her into his arms.

It was as though she had been waiting for this kiss for a thousand lifetimes. Yet she could never have guessed at its magical effect on her. It seemed to lift her up bodily and carry her off to the stars. It filled her whole being with a sense of blissful wonder, a feeling of completeness, a sense of oneness with the universe. And yet, at the same time, it seemed to turn her inside out, igniting every nerve-end with a fierce, pulsing hunger that tore like sharp claws, impatient to be satisfied.

And she had never felt anything like that before either.

His lips were the most delicious, the most exciting she had ever tasted, the strong arms that held her the most irresistible she had ever known, and she had never experienced anything half as gloriously intoxicating as the hard, virile body that was pressed against her own. Breathlessly, she clung to him in the face of the earthquake that possessed her, and it felt as though, in the space of a trembling heartbeat, she'd been torn apart and put back together again. Reborn.

As Matthew drew back and looked down at her he was experiencing a little of the same. The soft, pliant way she had melted into his arms and the fierce, hot passion he had felt in her kiss had, quite literally, taken his breath away. And he was filled now with an even stronger sense of urgency to do what he had come here with the intention of doing.

He bent to kiss her again, drinking in the sweet scent of her, his hands caressing the soft, feminine curves of her body. Then he paused and held her close to him. In a low voice he said, 'Maybe this is the moment to try and explain things to you. It's time I put you right about me and Claire.' And as he felt her suddenly stiffen he knew he was right. He must wait not a moment longer. This had to be done.

He took her hand and kissed it. 'Let's go and sit down over there.' He nodded to a wooden bench a few steps away, by the lake's edge. 'Come on,' he told her. 'This is important.'

Caterina allowed him to lead her to the bench and sat down, though she was not at all certain that she wanted to hear what he had to say. She'd been doing such a good job of keeping Claire from her mind and this sudden intrusion was like a bad taste in her mouth. Though what really distressed her was the sudden fear inside her that she would be unable to believe what he was about to tell her.

Matthew seated himself beside her, taking both of her hands in his so that the two of them were facing one another. And from the intense look in his eyes it was perfectly clear that he was absolutely determined to convince her. She felt another flicker of fear. This felt like a test of some description. He was about to ask her to trust him and she wasn't certain if she dared.

'It's a tricky situation, but really it's very simple.' Matthew continued to hold her hands as he began his explanation, his eyes never for one moment leaving her face. 'What I told you before is true, in spite of appearances. Claire and I are no longer involved in any way. Our relationship ended three months ago.'

Caterina did not say a word. It was not necessary to put into words the scepticism that was written all over her face.

Matthew continued, 'Before you can understand you have to try and understand Claire a bit. At times she can be a little mad. She likes to shock people. To stir things up and create a bit of drama. She gets a lot of pleasure out of that.'

Caterina's expression never altered. She said in a monotone, 'I take it you're referring to that evening at your house? Well, I can't think why she would want to stir things up and shock me.'

'Because you were there. Because of who you are—'

'You mean she knew who I was?' Caterina couldn't resist cutting in. 'I didn't think she even realised I was there! She never even looked at me. I felt I'd become invisible!'

She wished instantly that she hadn't said that. It had sounded peevish and it had been revealing. It had revealed just how much that little scene had got to her and she would have preferred him to believe that it hadn't touched her at all.

'Yes, I'm sorry she was rude, on top of everything else. She does have a habit of forgetting her manners.' Matthew paused and squeezed her hands. 'But what I'm trying to tell you is that what happened that evening was just a silly game. All that stuff about "Come back to bed" and so on. She only did it to amuse herself and in order to shock you.'

The more of this story she was forced to hear, the more miserable Caterina was becoming. How could he expect her to believe such a preposterous invention?

She said in a scathing tone, 'Oh, yes, and I suppose the only reason she was in your bedroom dressed in nothing but her knickers and bra was because she'd dropped by to give you a hand sorting out your sock drawer?'

'She wasn't in my bedroom.' Matthew shook his head with a wry smile. 'When I came downstairs to greet you she was in the bathroom. I was getting changed, just about to take her back to her hotel. She was not in my room. There was nothing going on.'

Caterina was trying very hard to get her head round this story, but it just didn't add up. She tried to pull her hands away.

'Look,' she said impatiently, 'we're just wasting our time here. And it really doesn't matter to me what the two of you were up to.'

And she was about to rise to her feet and walk away from him, though she felt so sick and torn inside that she wondered if she would make it.

But she was going nowhere anyway. 'Oh, no, you don't!' As she tried to jerk away, Matthew's grip simply tightened. 'This is important, Caterina. You've got to believe me.'

Her name on his lips never failed to affect her. It did so now. About to protest again, she faltered. Reluctantly, she remained where she was and listened as he went on, 'Like I said, Claire and I broke up three months ago—not that it was ever a particularly committed relationship anyway. It was more of a casual diversion for both of us. Claire can be a lot of fun when she's not being childish.

'But then a few months ago she got involved with someone else—some American in Chicago—and that was the end of it as far as I was concerned. Not that I was mad or anything. To be honest, I was more relieved. But one thing I happen to have strong views on is fidelity. I don't expect any woman to have to share me and there's no way I would ever dream of sharing any woman with another man.'

As he paused and looked at her his eyes were fierce and full of emotion. And the remark had been so heartfelt that Caterina believed him. She found that she was listening a little more closely now and that some of the brittle defensiveness deep inside her had disappeared.

Matthew continued, 'Claire, evidently, has different ideas, and she wasn't at all pleased at the way I so easily relinquished her. She started phoning me up, even flying over to see me and turning up out of the blue on my doorstep from time to time in a ridiculous campaign to persuade me to resume our affair.'

'And that was how she came to be at your house the other evening?' Caterina was still doubtful, but not as doubtful as a moment ago. Maybe, just maybe, what he was telling her was true.

'She turned up unexpectedly after I got home late from work.'

Feeling the tension in her soften, Matthew slackened his grip. And he smiled to himself. It was working. She almost believed him.

He went on, squeezing her fingers as though to encourage her to believe more, 'I was furious and I told her so. She got upset and started to cry. And that was why she ended up in the bathroom—fully dressed, I can assure you—to fix her make-up. In the meantime,

I was in my room quickly changing out of my business suit, planning, as soon as she emerged, to drive her back to her hotel...'

He pulled a face. 'But then you turned up, and, well, you know what happened after that.'

'You mean...'

'I mean, my dear Caterina, that I was as surprised as you were when she appeared half-naked at the top of the stairs. I was also, as it happens, as mad as hell.'

Caterina frowned and tried to remember if he had looked as mad as hell. But she hadn't really been paying much attention to him, she recalled. All her attention had been fixed on the half-naked Claire.

'It's important to me that you believe me.' His tone was urgent, his expression serious. 'It's important to me that you know there's no other woman in my life.' With one hand he reached out and cupped her chin and let his gaze drift over her face for a moment. And there was such warmth in that gaze, so much subdued passion, that Caterina felt her heart quiver helplessly inside her.

Then it quivered again as he added, still watching her, 'I don't know how you feel about things between us, but I have a very strong feeling that something rather special is happening.'

Did he really? Caterina looked back at him. She felt all twisted up with confusion. Dared she trust him? If she trusted him, would she simply be heading for another fall?

These questions were far too big to answer right now. She dropped her eyes to her hands, which were held softly in his, noticing again what perfect hands he had. She felt a thrust of emotion deep inside her.

How desperately she wanted him. How she longed to feel those hands caress her naked flesh.

She looked up at him with a sigh. 'I don't know. I really don't know.'

'That's OK.' He leaned forward and kissed her face softly. 'Just so long as you believe what I've told you about Claire?'

Caterina nodded. 'I think I do.'

And as she suddenly smiled Matthew smiled back at her and relaxed at last. There were a few more battles to be fought yet, but perhaps this one was won.

For a moment he watched her, feeling a warm glow inside him. Then he glanced at his watch. 'Maybe we should be getting back to the party...?'

As she nodded he stood up, drawing her with him, then he slipped his arms around her and pulled her close again. 'But not,' he said, 'without one final kiss.'

There was no resistance in her now. Caterina raised her face to his, feeling her stomach turn to liquid as his lips pressed down on hers. And when they walked back to the party, hand in hand, a few minutes later, it seemed to her that she could see the future very clearly. She might fight it, but in the end she would lose herself to this man. Totally. As she had never in her life been lost before.

And as she dwelt on this prospect it was very hard to know which of the two was greater: her giddy excitement or her fear.

Over the next few days Caterina and Matthew spent every moment they could together. Working, eating, talking, laughing. And every single moment, for Caterina, was like a miracle.

She was getting to know a few things about him now—his likes and dislikes, his views on this and that—though he was maddeningly evasive when it came to answering her questions about his family.

Maybe there was something in his background that he was ashamed of, Caterina thought, remembering what Orazio had told her. And she was tempted to tell him that there was no need, that it wouldn't matter to her, but in the end she decided to say nothing. After all, there was no hurry. She would find out in good time.

For he had been right. Something was very definitely happening between them.

At least, it's happening to me, Caterina reflected. For it seemed to her that she thought about him constantly. The way he looked. The things he said. The sound of his voice. How it felt when he touched her. The thrill of his lips. And how kisses and caresses were simply not enough.

For there had been no real intimacy between them. She had yet to feel those hands caress her naked flesh. And the reason why this was so was, very simply, because every time they drew close to the brink she would step back. She did not dare to surrender totally, though she longed to, desperately. Her need for him was like a gnawing hunger inside her. But she knew what would happen. If she slept with him she would be done for. And that thought simply terrified her to the roots of her soul.

She believed him about Claire, who seemed to have disappeared from the scene. And she felt sure in her heart that she had nothing else to fear. All those slanders had been just that. He was not a social climber. He was not out to use her. She was not just a stepping-stone.

But still a mote of fear remained, though she longed to overcome it. It could do them no good. It was essential that she trust him. If she didn't, she would simply end up ruining their relationship. But until she could make that leap of faith she just dared not sleep with him.

Matthew hadn't tried to push her, though with each day that passed Caterina was certain that she could sense a growing impatience in him. And then a couple of nights before the garden party the whole thing came to a head.

They'd had dinner at a quiet restaurant overlooking the bay and were chatting over coffee when suddenly Matthew proposed, 'How about going back to my place for a brandy?'

Caterina could hardly bear to look at him. She was dying to say yes. Sparks of sexual electricity had been flying between them all evening. But she forced back her longing and said, swallowing hard, 'Not tonight. Maybe some other time.'

'OK.'

That was all he said, but with a coolness that chilled her, and a little later, when he drove her home, his goodnight kiss was almost chaste.

He's sick of me, Caterina decided. And no wonder. Who can blame him? She was sick of herself. Her whole being ached for him, yet she was insisting on behaving like a fifteen-year-old virgin.

She climbed out of the car and walked across the courtyard, feeling as though her insides were being torn to pieces. And as she stepped through the doorway then turned for a final wave, only to see the silver Jaguar already disappearing down the drive, she literally felt like weeping with frustration. For by walking away she had only made her longing stronger. It was no good. She simply could not control it.

And neither could she bear it a single second longer, she decided as she made her way through the corridors to her rooms. She turned sharply on her heel. I'm going back to him, she decided. I can't keep this up. I've simply got to trust him. And she almost ran all the way back down to the courtyard and virtually threw herself into her little red Honda.

She had a flash of renewed doubt when she reached the front door of his villa and stood poised to press her fingers against the doorbell. There was still time to back out, still time to cut and run. If she turned and fled now he would never even know that she'd come.

But she took a deep breath and pressed the bell firmly instead.

As she waited, she held her breath. If the maid answered, what would she say? Then, as she heard footsteps approaching, near panic possessed her. Would she live to regret this? Was she making a grave mistake? Should she make her escape now before it really was too late?

But a moment later when the door opened she was still standing there on the doorstep, and her heart flooded with joy and terror as she looked into Matthew's face.

She opened her mouth to speak, but no sound came out. Then Matthew stepped forward and held out his hand to her.

He smiled.

'Come on in,' he said.

# CHAPTER EIGHT

CATERINA stepped into the hallway and into Matthew's arms.

He brushed his lips against her hair. 'Welcome,' he told her. 'Welcome, my love. I was praying that you'd come.'

And in that moment all her fears and anxieties and doubts melted away like snowflakes in the sun. She looked up into his eyes. 'I couldn't stay away,' she told him. 'I just couldn't bear to stay away a moment longer.'

Matthew held her for a moment and bent to kiss her softly, her hair, her lips, her eyes, her throat. And she clung to him, kissing him back, drunk with dizzy elation, her arms around his neck, her body pressing against him. If this was madness, she didn't care. She would take her chances. But how could something be wrong that felt so totally right?

'Shall we go upstairs?'

He looked deep into her eyes, as though offering her the opportunity to change her mind if she wished. But there was no danger of that. Caterina nodded. 'Yes. Let's.' There was nothing she wanted more than to be loved by this man.

Without a word, he took her hand and led her up the marble staircase, and as they reached the bedroom door, which was standing half-open, giving a tantalising glimpse of the softly lit room beyond, he paused again to kiss her, holding her against him with a fierceness and a passion that made her heart stand still.

'My dear Caterina. How wonderful you are. The most wonderful girl in the whole wide world.'

Did he mean that? Caterina looked back at him, giddy, completely under his spell. And you, she thought weakly, are the most wonderful man. Then as he kissed her again, sending a knife of desire through her, she clung to him, caressing his hard shoulders with her fingers, suddenly totally sure of the impulse that had brought her here.

'Matthew,' she murmured against his lips. 'Matthew, make love to me.'

He looked into her eyes with a passion that burned her. Then, making her gasp, he was sweeping her up into his arms and carrying her bodily into the bedroom.

It was a big room, all blue and gold, with a vast bed in the centre—which was really the only thing that Caterina was aware of. He crossed to it and laid her down on it, then bent over to kiss her again.

'You're sure about this?' he said, brushing her hair with his lips.

Caterina nodded. 'Very, very sure,' she told him. And she reached up and slipped her arms round his neck, kissing his face, making him her prisoner.

He smiled then and lay down on the bed beside her, leaning over her, bending to kiss her. She was wearing a pink cotton shirtdress and he began to undo the buttons. Slowly, sensuously, his eyes never leaving hers. And just that simple action was turning her stomach to jelly. Desire, like a coiled spring, was tightening inside her, sending a helpless throb of longing through her, a sweet, burning tension that ached for release. And as he undid the last button and the front of her dress fell open, so that suddenly she was lying there in just her bra and briefs, she sighed and shivered with anticipation. She couldn't wait for him to strip the bra and briefs away.

But Matthew was in no hurry.

He looked down at her for a moment. 'How beautiful you are.' And he bent to kiss her stomach, making the spiral inside her tighten even more.

Still without hurrying, he raised her gently from the bed, slipped the dress from her shoulders and tossed it onto the floor. Then he was unhooking her bra, tantalisingly slowly, and freeing her breasts from the lacy white cups before reaching out to capture the aching flesh in his palms, grazing the hard nipples with the heels of his hands, sending a fire like a lightning bolt piercing through her loins.

Trembling, Caterina looked up at him as he tossed the bra aside and bent now to take one burning nipple in his mouth. This, she thought weakly, was going to be something special. He had the slow, sensuous touch of a sure and accomplished lover, and he was tuning her the way a musician tuned an instrument, plucking her senses, making them sing. She felt a sword-thrust of anticipation in the pit of her stomach. This was to be no hurried, fumbled coupling. This was to be like nothing she had ever imagined even in her dreams.

Matthew took her hand and laid it on his chest, inviting her to undo the buttons of his shirt. And as she undid them, one by one, she could feel his heart pounding, in perfect rhythm with the wild pounding of her own. As the last button came undone she pulled the shirt-front open and laid her lips, and her tongue, against his bare flesh.

He was slipping off her briefs now, she tugging at his trousers. And then, at last, they were lying naked together, limbs entwined, exchanging hot kisses, caressing one another with growing urgency, heading towards the climax that was slowly gathering.

But still he made her wait, and the growing tension within her was by far the sweetest torture that Caterina had ever known. I shall die, she kept thinking, if he makes me wait much longer. She could feel the hardness of him pressing against her belly like a rod, teasing, tantalising, driving her mad.

But when the moment finally came that she truly couldn't wait another second and she was beginning to feel she might end up drowning in her own passion he seemed to sense it and took pity on her, or perhaps he simply couldn't wait any more either. He lowered himself on top of her and as she parted her legs eagerly he kissed her hard and entered her in one piercing stroke.

Caterina arched her back in welcome and pressed against him. 'Oh, Matthew!' she sighed.

She was his at last.

It was a long, blissful night, though too brief for Caterina.

They made love again after that first time, even more slowly, even more erotically than before. Then they just lay together, kissing and caressing, each exulting in the warmth and responsiveness of the other's body, not needing to speak, for they had surpassed the need to speak. They had adopted the far more articulate language of the flesh.

And the depth of emotion that she felt for him as she lay there listening to the soft sound of his breathing shocked Caterina a little. I love him, she thought. For what she had feared, of course, had happened. She was lost. Without hope. Though it no longer scared her. She had never known it could be so beautiful to feel so deeply for another human being.

At last they fell asleep, arms wrapped round one another, and when Caterina awoke at his side early next morning it was with a wonderful, glowing sense of fulfilment. Looking at him as he lay there, still asleep, breathing softly, she found it hard to believe that she hadn't loved him all her life.

And it was at that moment, almost as though he'd sensed her feelings, that Matthew opened his eyes and turned his head, with a smile, to look at her.

'Well, look who it is,' he said. 'My favourite lady.' And he reached up and planted a soft kiss on her lips.

Caterina kissed him back. 'Hi,' she answered. And suddenly, as all her love for him seemed to rush up inside her, she was seized by a terrifying sense of naked vulnerability. All her carefully banished fears stood before her once again. It's hopeless, I adore him, she thought with a pang. If he turns out to be less than I believe he is, I shall die.

'And how are you this morning?'

He reached up and stroked her face, brushing the glossy light brown hair back from her temples. The touch of his fingers sent tongues of fire through her. She turned her head shyly and kissed the inside of his arm, pushing away her fears—for hadn't she resolved that she must trust him?—and concentrating instead on the clean, earthy scent of him that seemed to intoxicate her senses.

'Pretty good,' she replied. Thanks to you, she might have added. For she had never felt so gloriously alive in her life. 'And how about you?' she wanted to know. 'Are you feeling ready to face the day?'

Matthew smiled again and slid his hand round the back of her neck, so that she leaned back against it, feeling warm shivers down her spine.

'After last night, I reckon I'm able to face anything.' He let his eyes wash over her, dark and intense. 'Last night was pretty special, wouldn't you say?'

Caterina nodded as her heart seemed to melt away inside her. Last night, she was thinking, had been more than just special. It had been totally sublime. It had been out of this world.

She smiled, weak with love for him. 'Yes, it was special,' she said.

He reached out for her then and enfolded her in his arms with an air of such gentle possessiveness and protectiveness that Caterina felt pierced to her soul with happiness.

Then he kissed her hair. 'What a lovely girl you are. Lovely and wonderful and sexy and exciting.' He paused and held her a little more tightly for a moment. 'No wonder I think I'm falling in love with you,' he added.

Caterina felt a crash inside her and resisted the urge to cling to him. Love? She felt dizzy, everything spinning all around her. Surely he could not have said the word love?

But he had. And now he proceeded to say it again as he drew back a fraction to look into her eyes. 'I mean it, my love. I think I'm a lost man.'

And I'm a lost woman.

The need to say it was almost physical. But she did not. She held back as foolish fear flared inside her.

But she would tell him, she promised herself, very, very soon.

Then he kissed her, a kiss that turned her insides to water. And as she clung to him and kissed him back, their bodies melting together, it seemed to her that her heart must surely burst with joy and love for him. Suddenly she was filled with a bright glow of certainty that the future would be good, that there was nothing to fear at all. He was everything she believed he was and much, much more besides.

And now the garden party was only one day away.

'In the evening, when it's over,' Matthew promised her, 'you and I shall go out for a very special dinner.'

They were in the silver Jaguar, speeding along the highway on their way to a meeting at the Bardi children's home. Caterina smiled and glanced across at the man she so adored. It seemed impossible but with every second she simply loved him more. Though she still hadn't got round to telling him that.

Matthew glanced at her with a smile, and added, 'So try not to eat too many strawberries in the afternoon.'

Caterina laughed. 'Not much danger of that, I shouldn't think! I won't have much time for eating strawberries! I'll be rushing around like a mad thing all afternoon!'

For she would be attending the garden party in her capacity as sister of the Duke. It would be her task to mingle, make introductions and chat to people, and generally make sure the guests were having a good time. It was a task she actually enjoyed, though this year, to be truthful, she would rather have spent every second of the afternoon with Matthew.

Matthew seemed to read her thoughts, or maybe he felt the same. 'I don't suppose I'll have much time for eating strawberries either. I'll be too busy making sure none of the marquees fall down and that nobody trips over the potted plants.' He took his eyes from the road for a moment, turning quickly to wink at her. 'But I hope we can manage to have at least one glass of champagne together.'

'I hope so too.' Caterina reached across happily and gave his thigh a friendly squeeze. 'In fact, I give you my solemn promise that, just for you, I shall briefly abandon my position as official mingler with our illustrious guests.'

And as she looked at him she was thinking, I shall tell him how I feel tomorrow, after the garden party, over dinner.

It was time, after all. Over the past few hours he had declared his growing love for her over and over. He'd made her the happiest woman alive.

They were turning off the highway, heading towards town now. As he negotiated a busy roundabout, suddenly Matthew said, 'Ah, that reminds me... Talking of illustrious guests...' He paused to flick a quick glance in her direction. 'There's someone I'd like you to introduce me to tomorrow. The German industrialist, Dieter Marten. I'm told he's a pretty useful sort of guy to know.'

He said it so casually, as though it were a request of no importance, that for a split second Caterina was about to simply nod and say OK. But then, as the words sank in, it was as though a cold hand had touched her. Oh, no, she found herself thinking, was this the thin end of the wedge? Was she just another stepping-stone after all?

For though Dieter Marten was indeed a top industrialist, as Matthew had said, he was also a renowned and tireless socialite. Everyone who was anyone was a friend of Dieter Marten's, from all the major Hollywood stars to the cream of Europe's royal families. To make his acquaintance and get on his guest list would be a social coup indeed.

She felt nausea settle like a cold dead weight in her stomach. Was this what Matthew really wanted her for? To introduce him to people like Dieter Marten?

But she hid her reaction. 'Sure,' she told him. Maybe she was wrong, she was telling herself determinedly. Maybe his request was perfectly innocent.

As they drove on, he changed the subject. He started to talk about the Bardi project and Dieter Marten wasn't mentioned again. But the damage had been done. Caterina's happiness had vanished. For deep down in her heart a gaping hole had cracked open through which whistled the icy wind of fear.

The gardens of the Palazzo Verde had been turned into a wonderland. As Caterina stepped out onto her bedroom balcony she let out a gasp of admiration.

A group of yellow and white marquees, where the food and drink would be served, had been erected at the south end of the lawn. But these were no ordinary marquees. With their scalloped fringes and big fat tassels, they had a definite Arabian look about them and they lent the entire garden a gloriously exotic air. And the arrangement of potted palms and banks of glorious flowers, which even now were being set in place by a small army of men, added an exuberance that brought the whole thing magically to life.

The man responsible for this transformation, of course, was Matthew, and she could see him now from her second-floor balcony as he directed the final touches of the operation—a tall, dynamic figure in light trousers and T-shirt. Even just looking at him made her want to weep with love.

She turned away with a sigh. She hadn't spoken to him this morning, partly because both of them had been extremely busy, but really because she thought it better not to see him. Last night she had barely slept. She had driven herself crazy going over and over what he'd said yesterday in the car.

Had it meant what she feared it meant? Was she being overly suspicious? Was he simply out to use her? Or was that only in her head?

By morning she had been no closer to finding answers, but she had been sure of one thing. She couldn't keep up this madness. Somehow she had to get through the day ahead in one piece. It was her duty as a Montecrespi, as a member of the royal family, to keep her sanity intact for the garden party. And so she had decided that she had no choice but to steer clear of Matthew. Seeing him would simply make her crazy again.

But she wouldn't be able to steer clear of him for ever. Sooner or later today their paths were bound to cross.

She glanced quickly at the French carriage clock on the little table in the corner. It was nearly one o'clock now. In just over an hour the garden-party guests would start arriving and it would be her duty, along with her two brothers and their wives, to stand in line and greet them one by one. And for that part of the afternoon she would be safe from Matthew. But after that, at some point, she was bound to bump into him.

She frowned into space. Well, she would just have to cope with it. She would avoid getting involved with him, keep any encounter with him brief. Somehow this afternoon she must hang onto her equilibrium. And in order to do that she must pretend that he did not exist.

There was a tap on the door and Anna came into the room, carrying the china-blue dress that Caterina was to wear this afternoon and that had actually been set aside for the garden party several weeks ago, so at least there would be no indecision today!

Anna smiled at her. 'Are you ready, m'lady? Shall we start getting you dressed?'

Caterina smiled back at her. 'Yes, I'm ready. Come on, let's get this show on the road!'

Three-quarters of an hour later she was on her way downstairs to join her brothers and their wives on the flower-bedecked steps at the entrance to the main garden. And she was feeling confident and at ease, rather looking forward to the party, all thoughts of Matthew carefully scrubbed from her head. She knew exactly what she had to do and she was simply going to do it.

'Hi, you're looking terrific! Nice to see you!'

Carrie, Leone's wife, was the first to greet her as she joined the illustrious family group on the steps.

Caterina smiled back at her and returned the compliment. 'Thanks. You're looking pretty terrific yourself. I would say married life very obviously agrees with you.' For it seemed that every time she saw her new sister-in-law she looked even happier, even more blissfully in love.

Carrie laughed. 'How could it not agree with me when I've got such a perfect husband?' And she blew a quick kiss to the perfect husband in question who was watching her out of the corner of one adoring eye as he exchanged a few words with his elder brother.

Smiling, Caterina waved across to them, then she turned her attention back to Carrie as the other girl added, discreetly *sotto voce*, 'Did you hear about Sofia? Apparently she almost didn't come. The word is there's been a major bust-up between her and Damiano.'

'Really? Oh, dear.'

Frowning a little now, Caterina cast another quick glance at her elder brother, who as usual was looking perfectly regal and composed. Could it be that the rumours really were true, then, she wondered, and Sofia had found out that he was seeing Lady Fiona again?

Feeling a thrust of sympathy for poor Sofia, she flicked a glance in her direction and raised her hand to wave a friendly hello. But though Sofia smiled back there was a tenseness about her and her lovely oval face looked paler than usual against its frame of gorgeous red-gold hair.

Poor Sofia, Caterina thought. How hard it must be for her. Just twenty-three years old, with a nine-month-old baby and a husband who was playing around with his old flame. She shook her head and told Carrie, 'Sometimes I could kill Damiano. How can he treat Sofia that way?'

The subject was dropped then, for one of the uniformed officials was signalling that the guests had started to arrive. And indeed at that moment a glittering fleet of Rolls-Royces, sleek Bentleys and yacht-sized stretch Mercedes were in the process of disgorging their glittering occupants into the courtyard at the side of the palace. In just a few moments the party would be under way as the great and the good from all corners of the globe—princes and sultans and celebrities and diplomats—began to file past the little royal group.

And it was a fact, though nobody had bothered to work it out, that if you'd laid end to end a single brass penny for every title, castle, swimming pool and mansion owned by the people at the party that afternoon your line of pennies would have stretched more than halfway to the North Pole. One thing was for sure: this was no common-or-garden garden party.

For the next hour or so Caterina was kept busy greeting the guests. And she was enjoying herself thoroughly meeting old friends and acquaintances, some of whom she hadn't seen since Leone and Carrie's wedding. Though she had one shaky moment towards the end of the file-past, when, turning with a smile to greet the next guest, she found herself looking at Dieter Marten.

With an effort of will she managed to keep her smile in place. 'Welcome,' she told him. 'It's lovely to see you again.' And as they chatted for a moment she took great care to keep all thoughts of Matthew from her head. The very last thing she would be doing was introducing the two of them!

Once the guests had all arrived the party really got under way, and, as some parties did, it just seemed to slip straight into gear. As Caterina moved around, mingling with the guests, she was aware of the happy, light-hearted atmosphere around her. Everyone was obviously having a thoroughly good time.

To make the whole thing even better she barely set eyes on Matthew all afternoon.

She caught sight of him from a distance once, quite unexpectedly, and had to hold onto her champagne glass very tightly as her legs seemed to turn to sponges beneath her. He's so gorgeous, she thought weakly, and I really do adore him. But she banished these thoughts instantly and turned her back on him at once.

The second time she set eyes on him it wasn't so easy. She looked up and suddenly he was standing right in front of her. 'Hello, stranger,' he said, and she almost fell at his feet.

But somehow she remained upright. She even managed a weak smile. 'Hi,' she said brightly. 'Are you enjoying yourself?'

'I'd be enjoying myself more if I could see a little more of you. But I can see how busy you are,' he added just as she was starting to panic, 'so I won't interrupt you. I'll let you get on with your mingling. We can have that glass of champagne we promised ourselves at dinner tonight.'

Then he smiled at her and winked. 'You're looking beautiful, as usual. That dress is the exact same china-blue as your eyes.'

A moment later he was gone and she almost felt like running after him, though really she should have just been grateful that he'd kept it short and sweet. He's so wonderful, she thought helplessly. I'm sure I'm wrong to doubt him. And she found herself acknowledging how much she'd missed him this afternoon and how desperately she was looking forward to dinner with him this evening.

But she pushed these thoughts away. She mustn't drive herself crazy. And, switching her brain back into automatic, she plunged back into the party.

It was just after six that the party finally began to wind down. The food had been cleared away, the chatter had died a little and some of the guests were starting to leave. Caterina waved off a departing group, then, suddenly realising she was thirsty, decided to go off in search of a glass of water. And it was as she was walking past one of the yellow and white marquees that, quite by chance, something inside caught her eye.

She hesitated in her tracks and took a couple of steps back. Surely she'd been mistaken? It couldn't have been what she'd imagined. She'd been seeing things. A mirage. It was really too bizarre. And she narrowed her eyes and peered inside.

Of course, she should never have done it. She ought to have walked swiftly on. For if she hadn't stepped back, if she hadn't peered into the marquee the world wouldn't have come crashing down about her ears. Because that was what happened as, her eyes adjusting to the dim light, she found herself looking at a scene straight from hell.

What she had seen was no mirage. What she had seen really was Claire—though she hadn't realised at first who the man with her was. But she could see clearly enough now and it was turning her heart to cinders. For the man Claire was kissing at this very moment was Matthew.

He had his back to her and had no idea that she had seen him. Feeling as if she might faint or be sick, Caterina lurched away from the marquee door and stood for a moment round the corner, catching her breath. Every inch of her seemed to be crying out in helpless pain.

Somehow she managed to walk away from the ghastly scene, her brain numb, her emotions seething inside her. And by some weird coincidence the first person she saw, as she made her way back to the party, was Dieter Marten.

'Dieter!' She walked up to him and caught him lightly by the arm. 'There's someone I know who's dying to meet you. Let me introduce you to him now.'

She would shame him, she thought wretchedly, as he tried to hide in the marquee with his girlfriend. She would carry out her introduction—which, it was plain now, was all he wanted of her—and then she would turn her back on him for ever.

It was only a short walk back the way she had come, though to Caterina's shaky legs it felt like a marathon. It was taking all of her strength just to keep herself upright and to keep on putting one foot in front of the other.

But at last they were nearly there. She turned the corner. And it was at that moment that Matthew and Claire emerged from the marquee.

For a split second the whole world seemed to tilt on its axis and Caterina felt as though she might actually slide off. She saw a dark look cross Matthew's face. She saw Claire smirk and toss her head. And suddenly she knew exactly what it must feel like to have your heart wrenched from your chest and thrown to a pack of wolves.

But she kept going. She even managed to smile a cool smile as she addressed Matthew as though he were a stranger.

'Mr Allenby,' she said, 'this is the gentleman you wished to meet. Dieter, meet Mr Matthew Allenby.'

Then she turned sharply away. She had to get out of here fast, before she collapsed and made a totally pathetic spectacle of herself.

A moment later she was walking swiftly back across the grass, a slender, shattered figure in a china-blue dress, looking for all the world like the royal lady she was but feeling as though she had just stepped off some cliff-edge and was plummeting headlong into an abyss as black and endless as the grief that filled her heart.

## CHAPTER NINE

CATERINA escaped from the party as soon as she decently could, threw herself into her car and just drove for half an hour. Then, high up on the coast road, she pulled into the side and sat staring blindly out at the horizon.

Matthew Allenby was a total skunk. A lying, cheating skunk. How could she ever have trusted him? When would she ever learn?

Of course he hadn't let her walk out on him as easily as that. After that scene outside the marquee he'd come hurrying after her, feigning anger at her reaction, trying to talk her round, acting as though he was the very incarnation of injured innocence.

She'd been at the edge of the garden, pausing for a moment to gather herself before resuming her duties as calm, carefree hostess, when he'd seemed to appear from nowhere right before her, startling her, a look like thunder on his face.

'Well,' he demanded, 'what the hell was that about?'

Caterina looked at him and felt her poor heart shrink to nothing. How would she manage without him? She loved him. She adored him. Losing him would be like a light switching off.

But as well as despair there was anger in her that he should have had the shameless nerve to come after her like this and try to talk her round with more of his lies. She fixed him with a hard look. 'Hadn't you better get back to Dieter? You don't want to keep such a valuable contact hanging around.' Every word was like a nail in the coffin of her love for him.

But he ignored her bitter reprimand and answered with one of his own. 'Have you taken leave of your senses to behave the way you did back there?' Then his expression softened slightly. 'Is this because I was with Claire? What on earth did you think was going on?'

What did she think was going on? The question was almost funny. But then he wasn't aware that she'd seen him earlier, before he and Claire had stepped out of the marquee. He had no idea that she'd seen them embracing.

She felt tempted to tell him, to throw it in his face, to prove that this time appearances were definitely what they seemed! But what would be the point? It wouldn't change anything. All it would do was prompt him to invent some even more elaborate lie than the one he was already planning to tell her. And she didn't want to hear his lies. She'd already heard enough.

So she glared at him, fighting the pain within her. 'Save the lies, Matthew. I really don't want to hear them. Go back to Claire. She's probably more use to you than I am. I don't want anything more to do with you. We're through.'

'Caterina...' He ignored that and took a step towards her. 'Caterina, calm down and listen to what I have to say...'

Calm down? That was an insult! How dared he tell her to calm down? He'd just torn her heart to pieces and now he was telling her to calm down!

Caterina took a step back. 'Go to hell,' she told him, though it was herself, she feared, who was really destined for that fate. All the tortures of hell were what lay ahead of her now. And as he started to speak again she raised her hands to her ears. 'I won't listen to you. Don't try to make me. You're wasting your breath.'

A look flashed across his eyes and she knew what he was thinking—that it would be so easy to take hold of her, to tear her hands from her ears and force her to listen whether she wanted to or not. But it was the wrong time and the wrong place and he respected her position. He would not humiliate her in front of all the guests.

And, indeed, he did not. With a shrug, he seemed to accept her refusal. 'Very well,' he told her. 'Suit yourself. You're free to believe whatever you choose.'

'Yes, I am.' She fixed him with scornful blue eyes. 'Now why don't you just go back to Dieter? You're wasting valuable social-ladder-climbing time.'

About to turn away, he paused then and raised a dark eyebrow. 'It was very good of you,' he observed, 'to go to the trouble of introducing me.'

'I like to keep my promises.' The words were an indictment. 'I said I would and I don't like letting people down.' As the emotion welled up inside her, the hurt, the sense of betrayal, she had to fight to keep her misery from her voice. 'No doubt you find it funny, but some of us are like that.'

He was as impenetrable as iron. He did not bat an eyelash. Her reproof glanced off him like a rubber arrow off a suit of armour. No wonder he was such a good liar. It was easy to lie when you had no conscience. And a barrowload of cynicism.

'I salute your integrity,' he told her. Then he made to turn away again, but paused at the last moment.

He smiled. 'However, your gesture wasn't really necessary. I'd already introduced myself to Dieter earlier in the afternoon.'

And, with that, he turned and walked off.

At first, Caterina had taken no account of that final revelation. As she'd gone through the motions for the next half-hour or so, playing her part as hostess, waving goodbye to the guests who were leaving, she really hadn't given it a great deal of thought. And as she'd climbed into her car and driven furiously up the coast road—in a rather erratic fashion, taking the bends like a demon—one of the reasons why she had wisely decided to pull off the road—it hadn't even crossed her mind at all. She'd been too full of helpless anger and despair.

But as she sat weeping in the car now, eyes fixed blindly out to sea, she found herself reflecting on it for a moment. He had introduced himself to Dieter. He hadn't used her after all. Knowing that took a little of the edge off her hurt and anger. The situation was not as black as she'd believed.

She stared intently at the horizon where a sleek white ketch glided, its two tall masts glinting in the sunlight. She had been wrong about that bit. Could she be wrong about the rest?

Yet how could she be wrong about Claire? She had seen with her own eyes the two of them locked in a passionate embrace. Tears welled up in her eyes. No, he was a faithless serpent. She was right to scrub him from her life.

But wait. Surely there was something rather strange, she was thinking, about the fact that Claire had been at the garden party at all? Surely Matthew wouldn't have invited her or even have wanted her there? If he was trying to woo her, Caterina, for whatever reason, good or bad, he was far too smart to have done something as gauche as that.

She frowned. It didn't add up. There was definitely something a little odd about it. And now she was recalling what Matthew had once told her: that Claire liked to stir things up, that she enjoyed creating scenes. Was it possible that Caterina had somehow stumbled upon such a scene?

She had grown very still now. Had she been too hasty in her judgement? Ought she to have listened to his explanation? Should she have given him a chance?

The tears had stopped falling and the ketch on the horizon, its sails turned against the light wind, was gradually coming into focus. She continued to stare at it. There was too much confusion in her brain. Too many questions. Too many blanks that needed filling in. And she'd been torn apart for too long now by too many conflicting emotions. It was time to put an end to it. It was time to find out the truth.

She could see the ketch quite clearly now, in every perfect sharp detail. And she could also see quite clearly what it was that she must do. She must go to the one person who could provide the answers she needed, the one person who could finally set her mind straight. And she must do it right now. She must not wait.

Feeling a sudden rush inside her of mingled love and fear and hope, she switched on the engine, turned the car around and headed slowly back down the hill. To Matthew.

\* \* \*

The first thing Caterina saw as she turned into the driveway of Matthew's villa was the low silver Jaguar parked outside the front door.

So he was at home. Relief and panic collided inside her. Finally, she would have the answers she needed to all her questions.

She parked her Honda next to the Jaguar and stepped out onto the gravel, her legs feeling like bales of straw beneath her. But there could be no backing down now. She was determined to go through with this. Win or lose, for better or for worse, when she finally re-emerged through the front door everything would be clear, her fate decided.

On that onerous thought she reached out and pressed the doorbell.

The door was opened almost at once by the same girl as before, who looked surprised as before and hurriedly sketched a curtsy.

'You don't have to bother with that. I've come to see Mr Allenby.' As she spoke Caterina was peering over the girl's shoulder. 'He is at home, isn't he? I saw his car outside.'

'Yes, ma'am, he's at home.' However, the girl did not usher her inside. Instead, she looked quite mortified as she added, 'But he gave me strict instructions not to let anyone in.'

Did he indeed? Caterina's heart was beating fast now as the girl stood apologetically, but firmly, in the doorway.

'Well, I'm sorry,' she said, 'but I'm afraid I have to see him.' And before the girl could stop her she was diving past her and darting across the hallway to the foot of the marble staircase.

'Where is he?' she demanded. 'Tell me where he is.'

'He's upstairs in his room, ma'am.' The poor girl looked quite horrified. And she looked even more horrified as Caterina began to sprint upstairs. 'Oh, heavens!' she wailed. 'I'll be in for it now! He told me most strictly that he didn't want any visitors!'

But it was too late for such protests. Caterina was at the top of the stairs, though as she reached the first floor and was about to head towards his bedroom she was aware of an involuntary fierce tightening in her breast. For suddenly she was remembering that first night they'd made love...

Him leading her up the stairs, then along the corridor. Pausing for a kiss outside his bedroom door. It had been the most beautiful night. The most magical of her life. And as sweet memories flooded through her she felt weak with sudden misery and almost turned on her heel and fled back downstairs.

But she gave herself a firm shake. No one had said this was going to be easy, but she had made a decision and now she had to see it through. Win or lose, remember? And, squaring her shoulders, her nails cutting into her palms like broken glass, she took a deep breath and headed down the corridor.

His bedroom was open and Caterina felt her heart falter again as she caught her first glimpse of the familiar blue and gold décor and the huge blue bed that stood in the centre. But she bit back her emotions and strode straight in.

He was not in the room. She felt a flicker of panic. Had he heard her coming and removed himself elsewhere? She hadn't thought of that before—that he might refuse to see her.

But just at that moment, as she was wondering what to do next, he appeared quite suddenly from his dressing room behind her.

'Well,' she heard him say. 'Look who's here.'

Caterina spun round and felt her heart crack inside her. Win or lose, she had told herself. But she must win or she would die. How could she lose a man as wonderful as Matthew and survive?

He had evidently recently showered for his dark hair was wet, pushed back from his forehead, as glossy as a seal's back. And he was wearing nothing but a pair of grey cotton trousers and an expression that was almost as black as his hair.

He said, 'How did you get in? I left very clear instructions.'

Caterina took a deep breath. 'I'm afraid I just walked in.'

It's hopeless, she was thinking as she took in the broad shoulders, the muscular, suntanned chest, every single glorious inch of him, and felt a longing as sharp as a sword-thrust pierce through her. She loved him. From top to toe. She loved everything about him. Even the frown between his brows, though it cut her heart to ribbons, was somehow special and precious just because it was his.

She pulled herself together and added, 'Don't blame the girl. She tried to stop me. But I just walked past her. I'm sorry, but I had to see you.'

He said nothing for a moment, just stood there and looked at her, and the expression on his face was impossible to read. Then the dark eyes narrowed. 'So why have you come?'

Caterina swallowed hard. At least it seemed as if he was going to listen. She'd been secretly terrified that he might just try to throw her out. She breathed carefully for a moment, fighting the spinning in her head, struggling to figure out the best words to explain herself with. But her brain was in a mess. She would have to rely on instinct.

She looked at him. 'I came,' she said, her mouth dry, her tone stilted, 'because I want to know the truth about what's going on. You see, it's all a total muddle. I can't get any of it to make sense. I wouldn't listen to you before, but I'm prepared to listen to you now.'

His expression did not alter. 'Maybe I'm not in the mood for explaining now.'

That closed look was killing her. It was like a knife through her innards. Caterina stood very still and tried to hold herself together.

She said, swallowing again, 'I'm sorry I wouldn't listen earlier. It was wrong of me. But I was upset. I really do wish you'd explain now.'

Again, at first he said nothing, and as the dark eyes fixed on her Caterina could feel herself going crazy. It was agony to look at him. She glanced away nervously, her eyes darting to the dressing table at her elbow—the set of silver-backed brushes, the china dish whose contents glistened.

Then, at last, Matthew began to speak, slipping his hands into his trouser pockets. 'OK,' he consented, 'you shall have your explanation. Though I must begin by saying something I've already told you several times—namely that appearances are not always what they seem.'

Oh, no, not that again! Caterina glanced back at him impatiently. 'I think I should tell you,' she informed him in a brittle tone, that I saw more than just you and Claire emerging from the marquee. I saw you a few minutes earlier. I saw the two of you kissing.'

To her surprise, his expression did not alter. 'I know,' Matthew said calmly. 'I already worked that out. But I can assure you the situation was not at all how it looked.'

No? Could that be true or was this a mega-lie she was about to hear? She said through lips so stiff that they scarcely felt as if they belonged to her, 'Then what was the situation if it was not how it looked?' And she darted her gaze away fearfully and let it roam at nervous random over the dressing tabletop.

Matthew was watching her. He could feel the tension in her. 'I told you before that Claire has a penchant for creating drama. Well, that's what happened. What must have looked like an embrace in actual fact was nothing of the sort. All it was was a bit of show on her part.

'I wondered at the time why she suddenly flung her arms around me. But it was obviously because she'd caught sight of you in the marquee doorway and decided to give you something worth seeing.'

Poor Caterina's heart was pounding against her ribs. This was exactly what she'd been hoping and now she was half-afraid to believe it. Keeping her gaze fixed on the dressing table, she said, 'I see. So it was just a piece of show on her part, was it?' She paused and licked her lips, which were as dry as paper. 'Maybe, just maybe, I might be prepared to accept that, but what were the two of you doing in the marquee in the first place?'

'What we were doing in the marquee was saying goodbye...'

He paused and, as he'd expected, the blue eyes did dart round then, though almost immediately they resumed their scrutiny of the dressing table.

'She gatecrashed the party, much to my displeasure, simply so she could have a suitably important setting to inform me that she was going back to her boyfriend in Chicago and she'd decided I was right—our affair was dead and over. The reason we were in the marquee was because that's where I'd dragged her after she accosted me earlier while I was speaking to some people. Knowing what she's like, I had no desire for a public scene.'

A half-smile touched his lips. 'Little did I guess that you were about to descend on us and witness the whole sorry farce.'

'I descended on you by accident. I wasn't actually looking for you.'

That was just in case he thought she'd been keeping tabs on him. But it sounded a bit cool and cool wasn't what she was feeling and she wanted to be as honest with him as she wanted him to be with her. She felt a surge of frustration. She was still so confused. Could she believe what he was telling her? She wanted to. Desperately. And all of her instincts were telling her that she should.

So why was she holding back? Suddenly impatient with herself, she looked into his eyes and found herself saying, 'I nearly died when I looked into that marquee and saw you. I couldn't believe it. After all the things you've said to me. And after what's happened between us... I mean, you must know how I feel about you... There's no way you can't know. It's got to be obvious... And when I saw you I just couldn't... I just couldn't believe it...'

As emotion overwhelmed her, she turned abruptly away. And as she stood there, heart pounding, she suddenly noticed something.

With a disbelieving frown she leaned towards the dressing table and peered down into a china dish of cuff-links. Surely, she was thinking, she must be seeing things? But she wasn't seeing things. She reached out one hand and carefully extracted one of the cuff-links, one of the gold ones with the armorial crest in blue enamel.

She turned curiously to Matthew, her eyebrows lifting. 'Is this cuff-link yours?' she demanded.

'I reckon it must be.' There was a strange look on his face. 'It was there on my dressing table, so, yes, I reckon it must be mine.'

Caterina looked down at the cuff-link again and then looked at Matthew. 'But this,' she informed him, 'is the coat of arms of the Duke of Weyland. Only very close members of his family are allowed to wear this crest.'

And she fixed her gaze on his face and waited for his reply.

It was delivered with his usual perfect calm. 'That's right too,' he consented. 'I see you know your English aristocracy.'

Caterina was barely breathing. Her brain was spinning in her head. She continued to stare at Matthew. 'And do you have the right to wear this crest?' Though even before he spoke she was certain she knew the answer. Suddenly all sorts of cogs and bits were falling into place.

He began to walk towards her, slipping his hands from his trouser pockets. Then, calmly, he reached out and took the cuff-link from her.

'These cuff-links,' he told her, 'were given to me on my twenty-first birthday by my grandfather, the Duke of Weyland. I don't wear them often, only on special occasions. And I guess I shouldn't really leave them lying around. They're not particularly valuable but they mean a lot to me.'

Caterina stared at him, wide-eyed. 'You mean you're the grandson of the Duke of Weyland?' She felt suddenly immensely foolish. 'Why on earth didn't you tell me?'

Matthew shrugged. 'Why should I tell you?' And he dropped the cuff-link back into the dish. 'My grandfather has numerous grandsons and I just happen to be one of them. I really can't see of what possible interest it is to anyone. The only person it's of any interest to is me.'

He was right in a funny way. It made no difference to anything. It was just that she knew now how ridiculous she'd been ever to accuse him of being a social climber. Good heavens, the Duke of Weyland was an even more ancient title than her own family's three-hundred-year-old Duke of San Rinaldo! It was one of the oldest dukedoms in the whole of England!

And suddenly she was remembering again what Damiano had told her—that there were a lot of things about Matthew that would surprise her if she knew them.

She slanted him a look. 'Does Damiano know?'

Matthew nodded. 'Damiano knows.' And then he smiled a small smile. 'But that's only because he had me so thoroughly checked out before he took me into his employ. I have every respect for him. He's a very thorough man, your brother. But I told him I'd prefer it if he kept my background to himself. I'm an architect. I get by in life on my professional skills. I don't need people knowing I'm tenuously linked to the Duke of Weyland.'

Tenuously linked! Caterina almost laughed out loud. Good grief! she was thinking. How about that for cool?

Matthew was standing in front of her. He took a step closer, and his eyes devoured her. 'But enough of all that. It's your turn to explain now. You said something a moment ago I'd rather like you to clarify.'

As he paused, he reached out and touched her hair with his fingertips, causing a shiver of wild sensation to trickle down her spine. 'You said I must know how you feel about me. Well, I'm afraid that I don't and I'd really rather like you to tell me.'

Caterina felt a crash inside her as she looked into his eyes, so dark and so intense, piercing her like lasers. And she hesitated for only an instant before she told him, 'Surely you must know that I love you, Matthew?'

And she smiled. At last she'd said it and it had felt so natural on her tongue and suddenly she realised how badly she'd been aching to say it.

But Matthew was not smiling back. His expression was deadly earnest. 'Are you quite sure about that?' He continued to touch her hair. 'What about Orazio?' he asked.

'Orazio?' Caterina smiled. 'Orazio?' she said again. It was funny but that name sounded as though it belonged to another life now. She reached out and with loving fingertips touched Matthew's face. 'I don't care about Orazio. I knew you thought I did. But you were totally wrong. I haven't cared for a long time.'

Then she took a deep breath and reached up to kiss his lips. 'And, anyway, I never cared for him the way I care for you.' She paused and looked deep into his eyes for a long moment. 'I love you, Matthew. With all my heart I love you. I never really knew what love was until I fell in love with you.'

As she'd spoken he had taken her softly in his arms, but before he could interrupt her Caterina hurried on, 'I didn't tell you before because I was afraid. I was foolish. I believed the lies Orazio had told me and I was scared that, if you really were a social climber, you might just be interested in me because I could be useful to you.'

She laughed a self-mocking laugh. 'I realise now that was ridiculous. But at the time, even though all my instincts said to trust you, after what happened with Orazio, all that stuff Damiano told me, I guess I was just too afraid to trust again. I—'

'Stop.' Matthew had laid a silencing finger against her lips. 'You don't have to go on. I understand,' he said.

And as he looked into her eyes his heart was swelling inside him with relief and joy and a love that knew no bounds. For he had loved her since that evening at the Bardi dinner, when on a wild, crazy impulse he had decided he must marry her. For that was what his plan had been, though there had been a few worrying moments when he had feared it might never happen. Not that he would ever have given up. He would have kept on fighting for her till he died.

He gazed down now into the face that meant the whole world to him. 'The only thing I need to know is that you truly do love me,' he told her. 'For I swear to you, Caterina, I love you more than my life.'

Caterina was almost weeping, her happiness overflowing. As he held her she let her head fall against his shoulder and slipped her arms lovingly around his neck.

'Oh, Matthew. Oh, Matthew. And I love you more than mine.'

Matthew kissed her then, a kiss of burning love and passion, a kiss that expressed all the devotion in his heart. And Caterina clung to him, scarcely believing that the miracle was happening. This wonderful man, at last, was hers.

Then she drew back a little to look at him, a curious frown between her brows. 'Were you planning to keep me in the dark for ever about who you really are?' Somehow she didn't care for that idea at all.

But Matthew was shaking his head. 'Only until I knew you loved me.' He kissed her. 'But from now on there'll be no more secrets between us. And no more silly misunderstandings. Which reminds me...the story about Claire... You do believe me, I hope?'

Caterina laughed and kissed his nose. 'I believe you,' she told him. In fact, in the past few minutes she'd quite forgotten about Claire, the one who had sparked off this whole confessional! But she knew without a doubt that what he had told her was the truth. Wasn't it more or less, after all, what she'd already worked out for herself?

Still, she had to ask, 'So when is she leaving for Chicago? I wouldn't mind going down to the airport to wave her off.'

Matthew smiled. 'She's already gone.' He looked deep into her eyes. 'In fact, by the time you and I have finished making love, she'll almost certainly have already arrived.' And he swept her up into his arms and began to head towards the bed.

Caterina laughed and kissed his face. 'What wonderful news. Though I hope this doesn't mean she's going by Concorde?'

Matthew laid her on the bed and smiled a wicked smile down at her. 'For all I know,' he said, 'she may be going by single-engine helicopter.' He bent and softly kissed her throat. 'How would you feel about that?'

Caterina laughed as she embraced him and ran her hands over his naked torso. 'I think I would like that very much,' she told him.

And as he sank down beside her she reached out and hugged him fiercely. She felt like making love to this marvellous man for forty days and forty nights!

Two figures, hand in hand, were standing on the terrace that looked down over the east-wing palace gardens watching the sun go down on the last day before their marriage. At least, one of the two figures was watching the sunset. The other one, Matthew, was simply watching Caterina.

He let his eyes roam over her lovely, adored face. Never in his life had he been as perfectly happy as over the past two months since she'd told him that she loved him. And never had any decision he had ever made been so right as the decision he had made at the Bardi dinner.

Suddenly feeling his eyes on her, Caterina turned to face him. She smiled at him. 'What are you thinking?' she wanted to know.

Matthew leaned over and kissed her. 'I'm thinking how much I love you.'

She kissed him back and smiled. 'What a coincidence. I was just thinking how much I love you.' Then she kissed him again and looked into his face, feeling a rush of blissful happiness curl around her heart just as it always did whenever she looked at him.

'How about a walk?' she suggested. 'Let's go and say goodnight to our swans.'

As they set off down the steps that led to the garden she slipped her arm through his and hugged it close to her. Everything was perfect these days. Life couldn't have been more wonderful. Her whole family had been delighted at the announcement of their marriage—especially Damiano, with whom she was the best of friends again—and now she had another family, Matthew's wonderful family in England, whom he had taken her to meet just a couple of weeks ago.

The scarlet sun was still hovering over the trees beyond the lake as they headed across the grass that skirted the fountain, so lost in each other that neither of them noticed the sad, pale figure who sat alone on one of the stone benches.

But Sofia saw them. She watched them and sighed. What I wouldn't give, she was thinking, to be just a fraction as happy as they are. How I would love to be like Caterina and have a man who truly loves me.

That thought was like a splinter twisting in her heart. It was useless to make such wishes. Damiano would never love her. It was that woman he loved.

Lady Fiona. So she must stop torturing herself and learn to accept that her husband was lost to her for ever.

But she could not accept it. She dropped her head into her hands and wept.

Caterina and Matthew were standing by the lake now, arms round one another, watching the swans. And, though she was totally unaware of the sad figure by the fountain, Caterina found herself saying, 'You know what I wish? I wish that every couple in the world could be like a pair of swans and stay together for ever, devoted to each other, just like my parents were.'

Matthew kissed her. 'And like us.' For he knew without a doubt that the love they shared would last for eternity.

Caterina knew it too. She looked up into his eyes. 'We're so lucky,' she said. 'I wish other people could be so lucky too.' And as she said it she did actually think of Sofia, who at that moment, brushing her tears away, was rising from her bench and making her lonely way back to the palace.

'You're a very special girl.' Matthew drew Caterina close to him, loving her generous heart, adoring everything about her. 'Loving you for ever's going to be the easiest thing in the world.'

'And loving you for ever's going to be pretty easy too.' She kissed him and gazed into those eyes that could melt her soul. 'So, this really is for ever, then?' she said. And smiled.

He touched her hair softly. 'For ever,' he told her. 'My wife. My love. My future. For ever.'

As he kissed her the sun finally sank behind the trees. The day was over at last. Only one last night remained. And then, when tomorrow dawned, for ever would finally begin.

\* \* \* \* \*

*Look out for Sofia and Damiano's story in THE DUKE'S WIFE. Coming next month!*

## MILLS & BOON

## Back by Popular Demand

# BETTY NEELS

COLLECTOR'S EDITION

**A collector's edition of favourite titles from one of the world's best-loved romance authors.**

Mills & Boon are proud to bring back these sought after titles, now reissued in beautifully matching volumes and presented as one cherished collection.

Don't miss these unforgettable titles, coming next month:

Title #5   OFF WITH THE OLD LOVE
Title #6   STARS THROUGH THE MIST

Available wherever
Mills & Boon books are sold

*Available from WH Smith, John Menzies, Forbuoys, Martins, Tesco, Asda, Safeway and other paperback stockists.*

# MILLS & BOON

# From Here To Paternity

Don't miss our great new series featuring fantastic men who eventually make fabulous fathers.

Some seek paternity, some have it thrust upon them—all will make it—whether they like it or not!

Starting in July '96, look out for:

## Mischief and Marriage
## by Emma Darcy

*Available from WH Smith, John Menzies, Volume One, Forbuoys, Martins, Woolworths, Tesco, Asda, Safeway and other paperback stockists.*

# An intriguing family trilogy...

### This summer don't miss Sara Wood's exciting new three part series–True Colours

Three women are looking for their family–what they truly seek is love. A father is looking for his daughter and either one of them could be she.

Things are rarely as they seem in Sara Wood's fascinating family trilogy, but all will be revealed– in True Colours.

Look out for:

*White Lies* in June '96
*Scarlet Lady* in July '96
*Amber's Wedding* in August '96

*Available from WH Smith, John Menzies, Volume One, Forbuoys, Martins, Woolworths, Tesco, Asda, Safeway and other paperback stockists.*

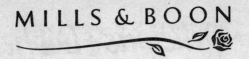

# MILLS & BOON

## Next Month's Romances

Each month you can choose from a wide variety of romance with Mills & Boon. Below are the new titles to look out for next month.

| | |
|---|---|
| MISCHIEF AND MARRIAGE | Emma Darcy |
| DESERT MISTRESS | Helen Bianchin |
| RECKLESS CONDUCT | Susan Napier |
| RAUL'S REVENGE | Jacqueline Baird |
| DECEIVED | Sara Craven |
| DREAM WEDDING | Helen Brooks |
| THE DUKE'S WIFE | Stephanie Howard |
| PLAYBOY LOVER | Lindsay Armstrong |
| SCARLET LADY | Sara Wood |
| THE BEST MAN | Shannon Waverly |
| AN INCONVENIENT HUSBAND | Karen van der Zee |
| WYOMING WEDDING | Barbara McMahon |
| SOMETHING OLD, SOMETHING NEW | Catherine Leigh |
| TIES THAT BLIND | Leigh Michaels |
| BEGUILED AND BEDAZZLED | Victoria Gordon |
| SMOKE WITHOUT FIRE | Joanna Neil |

*Available from WH Smith, John Menzies, Volume One, Forbuoys, Martins, Woolworths, Tesco, Asda, Safeway and other paperback stockists.*

# Delicious Dishes

Would you like to win a year's supply of simply irresistible romances? Well, you can and they're FREE! Simply match the dish to its country of origin and send your answers to us by 31st December 1996. The first 5 correct entries picked after the closing date will win a year's supply of Temptation novels (four books every month—worth over £100). What could be easier?

| A | LASAGNE | | GERMANY |
| B | KORMA | | GREECE |
| C | SUSHI | | FRANCE |
| D | BACLAVA | | ENGLAND |
| E | PAELLA | | MEXICO |
| F | HAGGIS | | INDIA |
| G | SHEPHERD'S PIE | | SPAIN |
| H | COQ AU VIN | | SCOTLAND |
| I | SAUERKRAUT | | JAPAN |
| J | TACOS | | ITALY |

*Please turn over for details of how to enter*

# How to enter

Listed in the left hand column overleaf are the names of ten delicious dishes and in the right hand column the country of origin of each dish. All you have to do is match each dish to the correct country and place the corresponding letter in the box provided.

When you have matched all the dishes to the countries, don't forget to fill in your name and address in the space provided and pop this page into an envelope (you don't need a stamp) and post it today! Hurry—competition ends 31st December 1996.

**Mills & Boon Delicious Dishes
FREEPOST
Croydon
Surrey
CR9 3WZ**

Are you a Reader Service Subscriber? Yes ❑   No ❑

Ms/Mrs/Miss/Mr _____

Address _____

_____

_____ Postcode _____

One application per household.

You may be mailed with other offers from other reputable companies as a result of this application. If you would prefer not to receive such offers, please tick box. ❑

C396
F